1 7 8

SEAL'S DECEPTION

TAKE NO PRISONERS

BOOK #8

ELLE JAMES

New York Times & USA Today
Bestselling Author

Dedication

This book is dedicated to:

My sister who still believes in me and encourages me to do my very best.

My daughters who help me brainstorm ideas.

My Beta readers: Susan, Fedora, Lynn D, Rosa and Amanda C. I love you guys so much for all you do for me.

Elle's Belles and Myla's Mavens who help me get the word out when I have a new release, as well as helping me make decisions about what's next. You guys are great and I love you so much!

Escape with...
Elle James
aka Myla Jackson

About This Book

Navy SEAL poses as a bodyguard to a sexy CIA operative undercover as the arranged bride of a Saudi prince in search of the biological weapons in the prince's palace

Ben "Big Bird" Sjodin, one of the biggest, baddest SEALs on SEAL Team 10 is tasked to work with a CIA operative on a special project with two of his teammates. All he knows is to meet his contact in a swanky bar in London. From there, he'll receive instructions.

Fired from INTERPOL for an affair with a double agent, Yasmin Evans has a lot to prove in her role as a CIA agent. Her goal? Infiltrate a Saudi palace, find vials of biological weapons of mass destruction, retrieve them and save the world. All with no more support than that of three Navy SEALs.

Yasmin's plan? Go undercover as the arranged bride of a Saudi prince with her three bodyguards. Once inside the palace, they will search for and find the deadly weapons. What she doesn't plan on, is the burning attraction she has for the bodyguard who could have been a Norse god in another time, or the Saudi familial factions determined to keep the prince from marrying his arranged bride. Inside an opulent palace, danger and passion flare.

Author's Note

If you enjoy reading about military heroes, read other books in Elle James's **Brotherhood Protector** and **Take No Prisoners Series**:

Visit www.ellejames.com for more titles
and release dates
For hot cowboys, visit her alter ego
Myla Jackson at www.mylajackson.com

Chapter One

NAVY SEAL BEN "Big Bird" Sjodin had to duck his six-feet-six-inch frame to get through the door at Night Moves, the exclusive underground London nightclub. His contact with the CIA had some pretty impressive connections to get him cleared to enter. The poor son of a drunk from North Dakota had no business being in such a high-class establishment.

Night Moves was the only place in the UK where the richest of the rich and the most popular celebrities gathered to drink, dance and partake of more exotic substances without the constant barrage of media and exuberant fans. Security was tight, and bodyguards swarmed the interior and exterior of the club to ensure the safety of the clientele.

Located in the heart of London, the building dated back to the seventeenth century and had sunk deeper into the ground over the years. Ben was used to ducking through doors. Having reached his full height at the age of fifteen, he'd had to be aware, or he'd end up with a constant lump on his forehead. Because of his height, he'd been called a lot of things: String Bean, Jolly Green Giant, and Stretch. Names never bother him, not even the nickname with which his buddies on SEAL Team 10 had tagged him. What he didn't understand was why three members of his team had been deployed to conduct a covert operation in the exclusive underground nightclub. Sting Ray and Irish waited at a nearby pub, topside. Once Ben made contact with his CIA counterpart, he'd be led to a safe location to be briefed on the mission and what it entailed.

More familiar with combat missions in the deserts of Iraq and Afghanistan, he was left confused by the London nightlife, nearly blinded by the reflections off the sparkling diamonds gracing the necks of the ladies in the room. Fortunately, he'd been fitted for a tailored black suit, courtesy of the CIA, although the patent leather shoes weren't nearly as comfortable as his combat boots.

None of this operation made much sense. Since when did SEALs team up with the CIA for covert ops? And, without a gun, he felt damned near naked. At least he had his knife strapped to his calf beneath his trouser leg. Not that he expected a celebrity to start shooting. Hell, he doubted the rich and famous knew how to handle guns. However, several stern-faced bodyguards stood on the perimeter who looked like they ate nails for lunch.

They didn't bother Ben. He could take out any one of them with his hand-to-hand combat skills. When bullies targeted him in high school for being different, he'd fought back by bulking up and learning self-defense. His size helped establish him as the guy no one wanted to mess with, even keeping his father from slugging him whenever he was shit-faced drunk and ornery.

Ben found his way to the bar and waited for a seat to open. In the meantime, he ordered a glass of water. Had he been out with friends, he'd have gone for a beer, but tonight, he was working. Until he knew what the CIA had planned for him and his contact, he didn't dare imbibe. With an alcoholic father, Ben never drank more than he could handle. He had a terrifying fear of turning out just like his old man.

Leaning his back against the bar, he sipped the water and nearly spewed when bubbles tickled his nose. *Damn Europeans!* In what universe did a man order water and get some carbonated bullshit?

He set the glass on the counter with a thump and glared at the room full of beautiful people dressed to the nines, laughing, talking and dancing as if they hadn't a care in the world.

Ben tugged at the knot of his tie, wishing he was back in his T-shirt and blue jeans. If wearing a confining suit and shoes without traction was any indication of what the operation might be like, he had half a mind to call his commander back in Little Creek, Virginia, and tell him to find someone else.

A blonde, wearing a short red dress that fit so perfectly it could only have been painted on, stepped up to the bar and nodded to the bartender. "Water, please."

"Watch it. They don't serve water here," Ben muttered.

"What do you mean?" The woman turned his way.

At first, her accent sounded American, with a touch of English and a flair of something Ben couldn't quite put his finger on—Turkish, or maybe Middle Eastern.

3

"It has bubbles," he warned. "If you don't like bubbles in your water, order something else."

She smiled. "It's sparkling, and that's the only way I drink virgin water." While she waited for the bartender to fill her glass, she turned to Ben. "You're an American, aren't you?"

He nodded, not really interested in continuing the conversation.

"Where in the U.S.?" she persisted.

Her voice was warm, like syrup pouring over his skin, melting into his pores. Ben tugged at his tie again, inclined to move away, afraid if he got started talking to the gorgeous woman, he wouldn't want to stop. He wasn't there to chat with a beautiful socialite; he was there to connect with an operative. "From all over," he said noncommittally, searching the crowd for anyone who might look like a CIA spy. Shit, what did a CIA spy look like? All this covert bull was well out of his league.

The bartender set a glass of sparkling water on the counter top.

The woman lifted it and touched her full, lush lips to the rim.

Ben's gaze followed, his groin tightening. Though she had blond hair, her brows were dark and her skin tones were more exotic. Blond or brunette, it didn't matter. She was striking and knew how to use her body to illicit a response. Yeah, and his body was responding. Damn!

He didn't need this distraction. If he was there to drink, maybe, but he wasn't. He was working. Ben straightened and took a step away.

Her hand shot out to clutch his arm. "Oh, don't go. Things were just starting to get... stimulating."

"Pardon me, ma'am. But I'm not interested." Ben peeled her hand off his arm and, again, started to walk away.

The woman's lips pressed together. She planted herself in front of him and walked her fingers up his chest. "Oh, come on, darling. Don't be such a spoilsport." She traced a line down his chest and snagged his hand. "Dance with me."

Once she had his hand in hers, she didn't let go. And her grip was surprisingly strong, for a woman. Instead of prying her fingers loose and raising a ruckus, Ben allowed himself to be dragged toward the dance floor and into the woman's arms. His gaze slipped around the room, still unable to detect which man might be his contact. Rather than fight off the woman, he figured he'd blend in with the crowd and have a better chance of spotting someone from his position in the middle of the room. He relaxed against her, moving to the music but ready to react at any given second.

Although tall and gangly as a teen, he'd always had a natural rhythm and moved well on the dance floor. He never lacked for a partner and often had his pick of the ladies for mattress dancing later. But Ben never stayed the night, always preferring to go back to his own place, rather than pretend a night in the sack meant anything by the next morning.

Long-term relationships weren't for him. And, God forbid, he should ever spawn children. With a drunk for a father, and a mother who hadn't loved him enough to take him with her when she ran out, Ben would bet his genes were hard-wired to be a lousy parent. Why inflict bad genes on a kid?

The woman in his arms rubbed every part of the front of her body against his, straddling his thigh several times in what Ben could only assume was an attempt to have sex on the dance floor. When he glanced around at the other dancers, he noted they were all pretty much doing the same.

"Sweetheart, loosen up." She wrapped her arms around his neck and mashed her breasts to his chest. "You're so stiff." Her calf slid up the back of his leg and her sex pressed against the top of his thigh. "Mmm...hard in all the right places." She leaned up on her toes, stretching to plant a kiss on his lips. "And so tall." Her fingers threaded through his hair, and she dragged down his head, making it easier for her to nibble his earlobe. "I've been waiting for a guy like you." She leaned back in his arms and glanced around the room. "Ever been to Africa, big boy? Wanna go to my place and get wild?"

Ben stopped in the middle of the floor. The code word for his contact was Africa. Body tensed, he frowned at his dance partner. "Been there. Done that. Got the scars to prove it," he replied with the required response he hadn't had to rehearse. Ben *had* been to Africa, and had scars from gunshot wounds to prove it.

He'd been to Somalia not long ago with his SEAL team. They'd gone in to decapitate the head of a Somali rebel group. When the operation went south, he and his team had been lucky to get out alive.

"Mmm. You can show me your scars, and I'll show you mine." She took his hand and led him across the floor, heading for the exit. Halfway there, she came to an abrupt halt.

Ben bumped into her.

"On second thought, I think another drink is in order." The woman changed directions and tugged him toward the bar. "Things just might get interesting around here."

As she reached the counter, she nodded to the bartender. "I'll have the Saturday Night Special."

The bartender glanced across the room, reached beneath the counter, pulled out a bottle of Jack Daniels whiskey, poured two shots and pushed them across the counter toward them. He wiped the bar behind the shot glasses and left the towel.

The blonde handed a shot to Ben, took the other and nodded. "Here's to getting to know you." She tossed back the whiskey in one swallow, grabbed the towel on the counter and spun toward the door.

A man entered, wearing a long black trench coat, his arm plastered to his side.

From the bar, Ben had a clear view of the doorway and the man coming through. He acted as if he had something beneath his coat, either strapped to his leg or resting against it. Alarm bells rang out in Ben's head.

"I'll take the trench coat, if you'll get the guy by the stage," the woman said.

7

"What guy?" Ben snapped his gaze to the stage where another man in a similar trench coat stood, his eyes narrowed, his arm against his side.

Fuck.

They carried rifles.

Ben nodded. "Deal. If you'll excuse me, I have some business to take care of." He clapped a hand around the woman's neck, dragged her in for a quick, hard kiss and released her. "Let's get wild later."

"You got it. In the meantime, knock yourself out." She moved toward the exit.

About the time the two men nodded toward each other and parted the lapels of their trench coats, Ben and the woman were on them.

"Got a light, mate?" Ben stepped directly in front of his guy, so close the man couldn't bring up the rifle beneath his coat.

"Bug off," the man said, attempting to step around him.

Again, Ben planted himself in front of the man. "Just asked a simple question. You don't have to get so..." He swung his elbow, catching the man's nose in a sharp upward thrust.

The guy grunted, and blood spurted from his nose.

"I'm sorry, did I hurt you?" Ben asked. "Here, let me help." He placed a hand on the man's shoulder and shoved him down hard while bringing his knee up at the same time. Again, he hit the man in the face.

Too stunned to do much more than stagger

8

backward into the stage, the man fumbled with the rifle beneath his coat.

Ben yanked the trench coat over his shoulders, trapping the man's arms to his sides. The rifle fell to the ground, the clattering sound drowned by the loud music.

With a quick kick, Ben sent the rifle beneath the closest table before twisting the coat up behind the man's back and glancing toward the front entrance. He didn't see the other man in the matching trench coat, nor did he see the woman who'd downed whiskey like Kool-Aid.

The wealthy men and women in the room only gave him fleeting glances as they twisted and gyrated to the music or went back to sniffing the lines of white powder on the glass-topped tables.

A bulky bodyguard narrowed his eyes and moved toward Ben.

Before the bodyguard could reach him, a woman teetered forward, bumping into the man Ben held in a vice grip

"Pardon me." She did a double take at the guy Ben was pushing through the crowd. She poked a finger into the man's chest and slurred, "You should have that looked at. You're bleeeeding." With a giggle, she twirled around and ended up on the dance floor, joining the other patrons moving to a techno-beat.

As he neared the door with his captive, Ben stopped short.

A group of people backed into him, and a woman screamed.

Rather than let go of the man he had in tow, Ben slammed the guy's face into a table, effectively knocking him out. He planted a chair over him and shoved a young man into it. "Stay here until I come back to collect."

The young man's head lolled, and he grinned. "Right."

Shoving his way through the gawkers, Ben found the woman in the red dress lying on the floor with the other man in the trench coat, her thighs wrapped around his throat, squeezing hard.

The rifle he'd carried in lay nearby. Thankfully, no one had picked it up.

"Need a hand?" he asked the woman.

"No. I got this covered. You might secure his weapon."

As Ben reached for the rifle, a burly bodyguard grabbed it first.

"If you know what's good for you, you'll give me that weapon." Ben nodded to the woman on the ground. "Otherwise, I'll turn my girlfriend loose on you."

The lady in the red dress unwound her legs from the man's throat, stood and smoothed her dress over her hips. "I'll take that, Wendell." She held out her hands.

The bodyguard placed the rifle in them, giving Ben a fierce glare. "Yasmin, you know this fella?" The bodyguard handed over the rifle and jerked a thumb toward Ben.

She grinned. "You heard him, he's my boyfriend."

10

Ben didn't know what the operation was all about, but he did know that the men they'd subdued had come into the club with the intent to fire off enough rounds to decimate the clientele. Had Yasmin not noticed them when she had, potentially every man and woman cavorting on the dance floor would have left the building in body bags.

Wendell gave a single nod toward Yasmin. "Thanks, lady. Anytime you need anything, you just call."

Her grin faded into a serious look. "I'm counting on it."

A couple other bouncers converged on Ben, Yasmin and the two attackers.

"We'll clean up the mess," Wendell said. "You might want to get out of here before the Bobbies arrive."

Yasmin gave the bouncer one last glance, hooked Ben's arm, and led him out of the club onto the cool, damp street in London.

"Did you know those men would be there?" Ben asked.

"I had received reasonably reliable intel they might make their move tonight. My counterparts didn't believe me." She shrugged and turned right, stepping out with purpose. "Guess they were wrong."

Ben hurried to catch up, curious about this woman who could choke the life out of a man with her thighs, get up and walk away like it was part of her normal exercise routine. For all he knew, that move could be.

11

"Do you mind telling me who you are, and why the Navy SEALs have been tasked to work with a former INTERPOL, now CIA, agent on a covert operation?"

"When we get to a safe location, I'll tell you what I know. In the meantime, keep your eyes open. Those two gunmen probably weren't the only ones scheduled to attack."

An explosion rocked the streets several blocks from where they were.

Ben stopped and spun toward the sound.

Yasmin's hand on his arm halted him before he could run toward the noise. "It's already done. There's not much you can do to help those people. By the time you get there, the police and ambulances will have arrived. You'll only be in the way." She took his hand. "Come on. We have an operation to kick off and no time to waste."

As if to emphasize her prediction, the wail of sirens sounded in the distance. People emerged from buildings, stared at the skyline and huddled in groups, whispering.

Ben tapped his ear bud communication device. "Connected with my contact. Moving to a safe location. Will report in when I know more."

"You weren't part of that explosion we heard, were you?" Irish asked.

"No," Ben said. "It wasn't anywhere close to us."

"Good to know," Irish responded. "So who's your contact?"

"I'll tell you when I know more," Ben said.

"Ha!" Sting Ray interjected. "He's a she. You dog. I'll bet she's gorgeous. Tell us where you are. I want to meet this sweet thing."

Ben tapped the ear bud several times. "You're breaking up. Contact you when I can."

"Breaking up my ass—" Sting Ray said as Ben turned off the earbud.

Yasmin glanced over her shoulder without slowing. "Your teammates?"

"Yup."

"I take it you're on a tracker, too." She ducked down an alley between buildings.

Ben hurried after her. "Yup."

"They'll follow."

Probably. As little as Ben had revealed, they'd be too curious to wait for him to give a location. Sting Ray and Irish would have the handheld tracker on by now. Ben's lips quirked upward. They'd be surprised by the beautiful woman they'd find him with. And, if they tried to sneak up on him, he might have the pleasure of watching her kick their asses.

Chapter Two

YASMIN EVANS HAD BEEN partnered with a multitude of men in various operations. None of the partnerships had lasted long. She preferred to work alone, but this particular operation required a bodyguard. Actually, several bodyguards. The woman whose place she was taking kept three bodyguards close at all times, until she'd slipped through their hands and disappeared.

Of course, the bodyguards hadn't had a chance after Yasmin got involved in helping the pretty runaway princess escape a life she had no intention of living. The young princess's escape at the same time as orders came down from Yasmin's boss had been fortuitous. The princess hadn't wanted to step foot inside the palace of Prince Khalid bin Abdulaziz, her fiancé by arranged marriage.

Yasmin needed access inside Khalid's palace. Luckily, she and the princess were of the same height and similar build. Yasmin had no doubt she could pull this off.

Now, to keep her bodyguard from getting in the way. Granted, it was *his* SEAL team that had discovered the problem to begin with. Yasmin supposed that was the reason the SEALs had been tasked with her support.

Still, she preferred to work alone. There weren't too many men she trusted. Her father had left her mother when Yasmin was twelve. When she'd been a brand new operative in INTERPOL, she'd fallen hard for her partner, French agent Pierre Marceau. Sadly, Pierre was a double agent for the Islamic State. He'd nearly gotten her killed before she'd figured out his real mission. By then, it was too late to salvage her career with INTERPOL. Thankfully, the CIA had a need for her services. Because her father had been American and her mother of Turkish descent, she had dual citizenship and spoke multiple languages. She'd gone to work for the CIA when no one else would have her.

Yasmin glanced behind her at the big SEAL easily keeping up as she dashed through the empty streets. Coming to a stop near the corner of two streets where a set of stairs led down to the underground railroad the English liked calling the Tube, she paused. A quick, but thorough, look around ensured she and the SEAL hadn't been followed. Without saying a word, she stepped away from the corner, descended the stairs and ran down a long corridor leading to the tube platform.

A couple of people waited for the next train, holding hands, whispering nervously. Yasmin could only assume they'd heard the explosion and worried about getting on the train.

Yasmin studied them for a moment, then turned and strode along the platform to the end.

A train slid to a stop. Weary people got off and hurried toward the exit. Others got on the train, and the area cleared of all people.

When the platform was empty, Yasmin leaped over the edge onto the gravel below, and followed the track, heading into the darkness of the train tunnel.

The SEAL followed. "You sure you know where you're going?" he whispered.

"No," she snorted. "I always lead my partners down dark tunnels in the middle of the night."

"Hey. No need to be testy."

"I didn't ask for a partner," she grumbled. "I consider you as having been inflicted upon me. I much prefer to work alone."

"Point made. But I'm on orders to work with you." He grabbed her arm and forced her to look at him. "I follow orders."

"Goody for you." She jerked her arm free and shot a narrow-eyed glance up at him. The light from the train platform shone brightly into her face. "I'm not so good at following orders." She continued down the track.

He dogged her footsteps. "Great. So where does that leave us?"

"Here." She stopped in front of a metal door, slid a key into the lock and then twisted the key and the knob, opening the door. Yasmin stepped into pitch darkness and fumbled for the light switch.

The rumble of a train sounded loud in the tunnel. A light flashed at the other end of the tunnel. The train.

The SEAL pushed through the door, turned and closed it. He bumped into Yasmin. To keep from knocking her over, he slipped his arm around her waist.

"Where is that damned light?" she muttered,

her hands skimming over surface of the concrete wall. A moment later, she found the switch and flipped it. A click sounded and the small room lit up. The furnishings consisted of an old metal desk, a couple of chairs, and a map on the wall.

"Welcome to my lair." Yasmin glanced around the room. "I do most of my work in London out of this office."

Her contact's lips twisted. "You call this an office?"

Yasmin frowned. "I do. It has all the right features: a desk, chair, electricity and even decent Wi-Fi from the café on the street above." She waved her arm around the tight room. "It's dry, for the most part and never too cold. What more could I want?" Her heartbeat stuttered. The small room seemed even smaller with the big SEAL filling it with his excessive height and broad shoulders. Yasmin dropped into the chair to put a little distance between her and the man who would work this operation with her. God, he was damned near overwhelming. Being with him in close proximity for the next week or so would be a challenge. Especially since she barely tolerated most men. "So," she said, her voice cracking. She cleared her throat and continued. "You and I will be working together." She held out her hand. "I'm Yasmin Evans. And you are?"

Holding his hands at his sides, Ben's brows dipped. "Thinking I got the wrong contact back at the bar."

"Oh, you got the right contact. I'm just not

sure you and I will work well as a team."

"Two others have been assigned to this detail. If you want one of them to be your primary bodyguard, say so, and I'll understand."

"No." She held up a hand. "You'll do." Hell, did it matter? Since her unfortunate dealings with the ISIS terrorist, she refused to trust any man completely. Hopefully, the Navy SEALS would be more honorable than a double agent.

He took her outstretched hand. "Ben Sjodin. Or Smith, based on my passport."

"How soon until your boys get here?" She tapped her fingers on the desktop. "I don't like repeating myself. We'll go through this once, and then we have to move on."

Ben glanced down at the expensive Rolex watch he'd been fitted with. "I expect they'll be here within the next two minutes."

A loud knock on the metal door startled Yasmin. She pulled open the desk drawer, removed an H&K .40 caliber pistol and pointed it at the door. "Open it, but stand back."

Ben's brows drew together. "Not if you're going to shoot first, ask questions later. It could be my guys."

She cocked her brows. "I guess we won't know until you open the door."

"Just don't shoot. If they aren't my teammates, I'll take them out."

Refusing to lower her weapon, she shrugged. "Just in case, I'll hold on to this."

Ben twisted the knob, yanked open the door

and crouched in a fighting stance.

Two bearded Navy SEALs stood on the other side, smiles spreading across their faces as they caught sight of Yasmin. Both men were almost as tall as Ben and equally broad-shouldered.

The man in front stepped inside, ran a glance over Yasmin and grinned like a fool. "Yeah. I see why your radio quit working." He stuck out his hand. "Ray Thompson. My friends call me Sting Ray."

She lowered the gun, ignoring the outstretched hand. The rumble of a train on the tracks rattled the door, the desk and the walls. "I suggest you get inside before the train hits you."

The man behind Sting Ray pushed past him and entered first, standing so close Yasmin had to lean back to look into his eyes. "I'm Declan O'Shea. But you can call me Irish." He smiled, but didn't offer his hand.

The two men crowded in with barely enough room to stand, their muscular bodies tightly pressed together.

"Let's get on with this briefing before we run out of air," Yasmin said. Already, their body heat had warmed the confined space by several degrees. "You can start by telling me what you know about the African biological warfare manufacturing facility you and your team blew up. Then I'll tell you what I know, and we can discuss where we go from here."

Ben turned to Irish. "You want to take it?"

Irish nodded. "On a mission in Somalia, we discovered a number of villages completely

19

decimated, the residents dead, but not from the usual beheadings, gunshot wounds or explosives. They'd died of something else. Then, in a palace located in an Ethiopian desert, we found an underground factory where they were producing biological weapons. They'd been testing them on the villagers in Somalia. Before we destroyed the facility, we learned vials of a highly contagious virus were sold to someone in the house of Saud."

"I don't suppose you could pinpoint a specific person or family, could you?" Yasmin asked. "The Saud family tree has a lot of branches."

Irish shook his head. "We suspect whoever bought the vials were friends, family or business partners with the man who owned the palace, Prince Yohannis.

Yasmin snorted. "That narrows the list down to a couple thousand suspects."

"It's all we had. We were just glad to get out without contracting anything," Ben said.

"Considering we're all in the same room, breathing the same air, I'm glad you didn't catch anything nasty, as well." She glanced up at them. "Is that all you've got?"

Ben and his teammates nodded.

"Okay." Yasmin opened a laptop and clicked the on button. "That jives with what I was briefed about and what we got from one of our contacts in Saudi." While she waited for the computer to boot, she pulled out a map of Saudi Arabia and pointed to Riyadh. "Our insider seems to think Prince Khalid bin Abdulaziz, or someone in his regime, purchased the biological weapons. We've been tasked with finding and destroying those vials before they can be used.

"The house of Saud won't let us waltz into its palaces and conduct searches," Irish said. "And staging an attack won't gain the U.S. any points as allies."

"We can't let what's in those vials be unleashed in the water system or any mobile population," Yasmin's fists tightened. "From what I've been told, the virus can spread quickly from person to person. If it gets loose, we could be facing a pandemic of epic proportions."

"How do you propose we get into Khalid's palace?" Ben asked.

"Walk in," she said and waited for their reaction.

Ben's brows puckered. "As some kind of peace-keeping delegation?"

The SEAL was kind of cute when he frowned. Yasmin pushed back that unprofessional thought and shook her head. "We wouldn't get too far inside as a delegation. No, I have a better idea." She clicked keys on her laptop and brought up a photograph of a young Middle Eastern woman: beautifully dressed, dark hair, dark brows, brown-black eyes and perfectly put together. Yasmin turned the screen toward the men. "*She's* how we get in."

"I don't understand, but I'll bite," Ben said. "Who is she?

"Princess Aliya. Prince Khalid's fiancée from an arranged marriage."

Sting Ray leaned closer to the screen and whistled. "She's hot. Is she going to let us into the palace? Is that the plan?"

"No, I am." Yasmin stared up at the men. "I'm taking her place."

All three men stared at her, then Sting Ray and Irish burst out laughing.

"You?" Sting Ray waved a hand toward her hair. "You're a blond-haired, blue-eyed westerner."

Irish's lips twisted. "There's no way you'll pass for a Middle Eastern princess."

Yasmin turned her back to the men then popped the blue contact lenses from her eyes. Setting those aside, she felt beneath her hair for the combs and pins, pulling them out, one at a time. Then she grabbed the front of the wig and pulled it off, shaking out her long, dark hair. When she turned back to the men, she lifted her chin. "What do you think?"

Ben's brows wrinkled. He glanced at the woman on the computer screen and back to Yasmin. "I don't know."

Irish stared at the laptop and then looked at Yasmin. "Has Khalid seen her up close?"

"Seriously, you don't look like her," Sting Ray said. "That woman's a total knockout with her dark hair and...and...well, everything." He held up his hands. "Don't get me wrong. You're not bad looking, but she..." He grinned. "She's ridiculously gorgeous."

Her fingers curled into her palms as heat raced up her neck and into her cheeks. "So she's beautiful.

You'll be amazed at what makeup will do."

"That's your plan?" Ben asked. "What if Prince Khalid figures out you're a fraud?"

Yasmin lifted her chin. "By that time, we'll have the vials and will be on our way back to London or the States."

"But, you're not Middle Eastern," Irish pointed out. "You don't speak the language."

Growing weary of their negativism, Yasmin pushed to her feet. "The princess grew up in England. She probably never spoke Arabic, either. But, that's where you're wrong about me. My father was an American soldier. But my mother was Turkish, of a minority who speaks fluent Arabic. I speak enough of the language to get by. Actually, I understand it better than I speak it, which could come in handy."

Ben shook his head. "It's far too dangerous to pull off. From all I know, Saudi royalty doesn't have a sense of humor, especially when it comes to their female subjects. There has to be another way."

Yasmin crossed her arms over her chest. "I'm listening."

The three men exchanged glances.

Ben turned back to Yasmin. "We can sneak into the palace at night."

"You need someone on the inside to get you in." Yasmin glanced from Ben to Sting Ray and Irish. "Any of you have another plan that will get a bunch of Navy SEALs through the front door of the palace? The fiancée of Prince Khalid will be allowed to enter, *with* her bodyguards. Unless one of

23

you wants to dress as the princess, my plan will have to do. Are we good with it?"

After exchanging sideways glances, the men nodded.

"I guess we'll have to be okay with it," Irish finally said.

"Sounds like you're set on this course of action." Sting Ray shoved a hand though his shaggy hair.

Ben drew in a deep breath and let it out. "When do we leave?"

"Tomorrow, around noon. I need to pack some of the princess's clothes and makeup and leave from her apartment in the morning." She nodded toward the men. "Ben will stay at the apartment tonight. Sting Ray and Irish can arrive out front when the chauffeur is scheduled to pick me up to go to the airport. From there, we'll fly out on the prince's private jet."

Ben's frown returned. "You've already arranged it?"

Yasmin grinned at Ben's look of consternation. "The princess's parents had arranged for the flight prior to leaving on a month-long cruise aboard their yacht. It's important we follow through on their schedule."

"How did you get the princess to hand over the keys to her apartment and her life?" Irish asked.

"She was going to run anyway." Yasmin shrugged. "I helped her slip away a little sooner. Aliya was more than happy for me to take her place. Now…" Yasmin stared at each man, one at a time,

"I need to know if you're in or not?"

"I'm in," Irish said.

"Me, too," Sting Ray seconded. "It's just the kind of seat-of-the-pants bullshit I love."

Ben's lips curled on the corners. "I don't look forward to spending time in a Saudi jail. But, I'm in."

Yasmin gave the men the address of the apartment and the time the car would be there to collect them. She gathered her laptop, jammed her wig into a drawer, plunked a wide-brimmed hat on her head and nodded toward the exit. "Let's go."

As the men moved toward the door, she added, "And watch out for trains."

Ben followed Sting Ray and Irish out onto the train tracks. No sooner had they all vacated the little room than the rumbling vibrations of a train heading their way caught their attention.

Irish and Sting Ray took off at a jog.

Yasmin locked her "office" and hurried along the track.

Ben kept up with her, glancing over his shoulder the longer the trek took.

Yasmin almost laughed out loud at the worried dent in his brow.

By the time they reached the platform, the train was screaming toward them. Ben whisked Yasmin off her feet and swung her up beside them.

Irish and Sting Ray reached down, extending their hands to Ben. He grabbed one each and was yanked up onto the platform.

The train swept up to the stop, brakes squealing. The doors slid open, but nobody got out. As late as it was, the city had settled in for the night.

Sting Ray and Irish headed for the exit to the street level.

At the last minute, right before the doors closed, Yasmin leaped onto the train, dragging Ben with her.

The doors slid shut and the train pulled away from the stop, leaving Yasmin and Ben alone. Her body still tingled from where Ben's big hands had grabbed her. She studied him from beneath her lashes.

Tall, blond, and incredibly handsome.

She touched a finger to her chin and circled him. "I don't know if Khalid will take charge of his princess and fire her bodyguards immediately. He might have men from his country identified to provide for her protection. We have to hope he won't replace her guards until the marriage takes place. Princess Aliya is known to have a blond hulk of a bodyguard. I think she ran off with him. If it weren't for the blond bodyguard, I'd assign Sting Ray as my number one."

Ben shook his head. "Sorry. Either I'm number one, or I'm out altogether."

She smiled. "Touchy much?"

"Not usually. But, I want to keep a close eye on you. I'm not so sure I should trust you."

Those gorgeous sandy-blond eyebrows lowered, making Yasmin want to reach out and run a finger across them. Then his words sank in and hit her square in the gut. Everything she'd worked for, every step she'd taken to redeem herself since she'd been fired from INTERPOL, slipped out from under her. That lead weight she'd carried around in the pit of her belly seemed even heavier. "You don't trust me?" Hell, most of the time, she didn't trust herself. Not after her fatal judgment of character had cost the lives of two French INTERPOL agents.

He crossed his arms over his chest. "Not particularly. Especially not with the safety of my men."

She nodded. "I get it. I wouldn't trust me, either." She pressed a hand to his chest. "You don't have to worry. I'll perform this mission without you. This is as far as you go."

Ben gripped her arms. "The hell it is." He pushed her up against a seat back. "As nutty as your plan is, it's the only one we have to get into Khalid's palace in Riyadh. The sooner we get to those vials, the sooner we get them out of the hands of terrorists or zealots. Some wars just aren't meant to be fought. Not this way. Not with the fate of the world at risk."

"Maybe that's what needs to happen. Let the biological weapon loose to cleanse the earth of the worst thing that ever happened to it. Humans." She shook her head and pushed against his chest. "I'm serious. I don't want you on this mission if you can't trust me."

"Look, I don't want anything bad to happen to my men. But I'm not backing down now. I'm just keeping an eye on you. Maybe, after a few days together, I'll learn to trust you."

She pulled out of his grip, her heartbeat pounding against her ribs, her arms tingling where his fingers had been. "Maybe, after a few days together, I'll just kill you, and we can call it even."

Chapter **Three**

BEN DIDN'T LIKE the whole set up. As tunnel lights zipped past the train windows, he couldn't keep the knot from forming in his gut. The more he thought about it, the more he was convinced they would get themselves thrown into some godforsaken Saudi prison. Or, worse, start an international incident between the U.S. and the Saudi royal family. "Tell me, does the top brass know what we're about to do?"

Yasmin shot him a look with raised brows. "Are you crazy? The American government can't keep a secret. So many leaks exist at the top level, we'd be insane to run it by anyone other than our small team."

Ben stiffened. "You mean you haven't cleared this operation with your boss?"

She shook her head. "My boss told me to get in, get out and make sure those vials don't fall into the wrong hands. He told me he wouldn't question my methods, and if shit hit the fan, I was on my own."

"Great." Ben shook his head, his gut knotting. "I'm all for storming into a primitive village or the war-torn streets of Iraq. But this is suicide."

Her chin jutted out. "I told you that you don't have to go."

"You're damn right I don't have to go. If we're

29

discovered, not only will I lose my job, we could end up in a shithole of a jail, rotting away for the rest of our lives."

She touched his arm.

An electrical charge shot through him. "So, go back to the States, or wherever you came from."

Ben stared at the hand on his arm, wondering why the hell heat was building beneath his skin, and knowing he couldn't walk away. "You're doing this with or without us, aren't you?"

She nodded.

He sighed. "And I'm betting we won't be allowed to carry a single weapon into the palace."

Yasmin smirked. "You'll be allowed one." She touched a finger to her temple. "Your brain. We have to be smarter and quicker on our feet than Khalid and his men."

Ben shoved a hand through his hair. "I'm crazy to even consider this."

"Agreed." She twirled a long strand of dark hair. "But, you're going ahead with it, aren't you?"

As he stared into her eyes, the potential disaster he was committing to whirling in his mind, he couldn't help wondering if her lips were as soft as they appeared. "I knew you were trouble when I first spotted you."

"You did?" Her shoulders relaxed a little and she smiled. "I knew you were the right man for the job when I spotted *you*."

"Yeah, yeah. Whatever."

The train slowed and came to a halt.

Yasmin glanced up. "This is our stop." The

doors slid open, and she stepped out.

Ben followed her up the stairs to street level. "For what it's worth, I like you better as a brunette."

"Really?" She shot a glance over her shoulder. "Why?"

"Makes you look smarter."

She came to an abrupt stop, causing Ben to run into her. She frowned, but her lips quirked upward on the corners. "I'm choosing to take that as a compliment."

"Take it however you want it. But keep moving. Someone's following us."

Frowning, she darted a look around him. "Already?"

"You're a princess. Get used to it." He gripped her elbow and turned her in the opposite direction. "Which way?"

"Two blocks north, on the left."

Ben hustled her toward the swanky flat on South Bank, overlooking the Thames. The man he'd indicated as following them turned one street short and disappeared. "Guess I was wrong about the tail."

Yasmin shook off his hold. "That's too bad. If someone was following us, I could only assume they thought I was the real princess."

"Did Aliya have problems with stalkers?"

With a nod, Yasmin arrived at the front door of the building. She fished inside her bra, removed a plastic key card and waved it over the scanner beside the entrance. The glass doors slid open.

Ben gripped her arm and escorted her through

the opening.

A security guard looked up from the telephone. "Give me a ring if you hear anything else about the explosion," he said and ended the call.

Tensing, Ben prayed the man didn't notice the difference between the extremely well-maintained princess and the straight-from-a-bar-fight CIA agent.

Yasmin waved her fingers and gave the man a hint of a smile. In a perfect English accent, she said, "Good evening, Seamus. How are you and your family?"

The man stared for a moment, his gaze scanning from her floppy hat down to her stilettoes before he responded with a smile of his own. "Good evening, Princess Aliya. I've never been better, although I'm wishing I was with me wife. She's taking the wee ones to Bath on holiday."

"Please tell me you'll be joining them?" Yasmin kept walking toward the elevator, chatting as she passed by the security desk.

The guard nodded. "I will, at the end of the week."

As Yasmin raised her key card to activate the elevator, the security guard stood.

Ben watched from the corner of his eye, ready to take on the Irishman, if needed.

"Pardon me, Princess Aliya," Seamus said.

"Yes?" Yasmin turned with a smile, the hat's brim dipping low over her face.

"You have a special delivery letter." He held out an envelope.

Ben stepped forward. "I'll take that."

The guard glared and jerked it away from Ben's reach. "I'm to hand it over to the princess."

Ben hoped when the guard did hand over the letter, he didn't get such a close look he'd figure out that Princes Aliya wasn't exactly who she pretended to be.

Yasmin squared her shoulders and turned toward the guard. "Thank you, Seamus. Nothing from my parents?" She took the envelope and tipped down her head, as if pretending to read the address.

"No, princess."

"Good. Have a pleasant evening." She spun on her heels and returned to the elevator, slipping her key card over the scanner. The doors slid open. Yasmin stepped in and Ben hurried after her.

Once the doors closed, Yasmin waved the key over the scanner, entered the floor number and let out a long breath. "I need to send my parents a card to let them know I'm leaving tomorrow. Please remind me, will you?" she said in the same accent.

Ben scanned the interior of the elevator, noting the video camera in the top right corner. Playing along with Yasmin's charade, he crossed his arms over his chest, squared his stance and nodded stoically. He assumed bodyguards were to be seen, not heard, unless the client was threatened in any way.

The elevator reached the top floor and opened into a small foyer. Yasmin stepped across to the broad black door and, once again, swept her card over the reader. A light blinked on the door, she twisted the handle, and the door swung open.

Yasmin stepped through onto posh, white shiny marble tile. The portico led into a spacious living area with floor-to-ceiling windows open to the night lights of London.

"Elaborate enough?" Ben muttered.

"My parents love me. Why argue with them?" She continued with the accent, giving a little nod to a camera installed in the corner of the living room, and another near where they stood in the entryway.

"They must care a lot about you," he said softly, playing along.

"Too much, sometimes. Like this wedding thing. They think I need to settle down with a prince."

"And will you?"

"I suppose I need to make up my mind by tomorrow. The prince is sending his plane for me."

"Is there anything you want me to do before you call it a night?" Ben studied the room for any other hidden cameras or listening devices. This was far out of his league as a SEAL, but Yasmin seemed perfectly at home taking over a princess's flat. "How long have you stayed in this building?"

She walked through the living area, came to a halt in front of the window and looked out at the view of the Parliament on the left and the Tower of London on the right. "A year and a half, I think. It seems such a long time ago that I completed my studies at Oxford. Be a dear and get me a glass of wine. Mummy and Daddy will be beside themselves when they discover I've fired the old bodyguard and hired a new one. Especially when they see you."

"Are you telling me I might need to look for another job tomorrow?"

She laughed. "Oh, heavens, no. If I go to Riyadh tomorrow, I'll want a bodyguard who speaks English, even if it's American English." She waved a hand toward the bar. "Please, the drink? Something dry."

Ben crossed the glossy marble tile to the black lacquer liquor cabinet and pulled out a bottle of Cabernet Sauvignon, wondering how much a bottle of the finest wine went for in London. Would it be considered grand theft if he opened one? He was even more curious how Aliya's parents would feel if they knew their daughter had alcohol in the suite. Most Muslims didn't drink. It was a sin. He located a corkscrew and popped the cork on the bottle, pouring a glass for her majesty.

His lips twitched. Wouldn't Yasmin love being called *her majesty*? He'd be glad when they weren't under constant surveillance. He felt like he was in a reality television show, waiting for the audience to vote him off the island.

"Pour yourself a glass, as well," Yasmin said. "I abhor drinking alone."

"I'm sorry, ma'am, but I don't drink on the job."

"Oh, pooh." She took the glass and flounced into another room. "Since you're working, take a moment to check for bogeymen beneath the bed and in my closet, please." She turned just inside the bedroom door with her hat still resting on her head.

Ben hesitated, unsure whether she was still acting or really afraid of bad guys hiding beneath the bed.

Yasmin tipped her head toward the bedroom and tapped her toe on the marble. "Don't just stand there. You work for me, now. I won't sleep well if you don't check."

Fighting to move with a casual stride, Ben crossed the room and entered the bedroom. Again, he hadn't seen anything nearly as opulent. The room was bigger than his, Sting Ray's, and Irish's apartments put together. The king-sized bed was the focal point of the room with its massive quilted headboard and matching satin duvet. A black lacquer writing desk stood in one corner and a deep red antique sofa in another.

Going through the motions of checking beneath the bed and inside the walk-in closet, he ruled out hidden menaces.

"The bathroom, please," she said.

Following her command, he stepped around her and entered the large spa-like bath area with a claw-foot soaker tub and a walk-in shower that could accommodate half of SEAL Team 10.

As he exited the shower, Yasmin stepped into the bathroom with him and closed the door. "Turn on the shower."

"Huh?"

"Turn it on, please."

When he didn't immediately respond to her command, Yasmin shook her head and crossed the floor, squeezing past him to turn on the water in the shower. Once she had, she faced him and spoke in a low voice. "Aliya showed me the cameras, but I haven't had time to check for listening devices."

Which explained the act from the living area through the bathroom. "Who placed the cameras?"

"Aliya said her parents had them installed to keep her safe. She rarely spent time in the flat, because she didn't like being watched all of the time."

"I don't blame her." His eyes narrowed. "I take it you've been here before?"

"A couple times."

"And the guard didn't recognize you?"

"I came as the blond-haired, blue-eyed college friend and made sure I never spoke or looked the guards straight in the eye. I memorized Aliya's accent and mannerisms. The dress and hat I'm wearing were from her wardrobe. When she decided it was time to make a run for it, we had a plan in place. She brought me the key to her place and a couple clothing items she knew the security guards would recognize. The rest she left behind for me."

"When did she leave?"

"Last night. She didn't take a bag or any of her belongings, knowing it would raise suspicion."

"Where did she go?" Ben asked.

"I didn't ask. She ran away with the bodyguard. I promised to stand in for Aliya when her fiancé set the date for her to go to him."

Ben crossed his arms over his chest. "So, when did you come up with this plan?"

"I got news of this assignment two weeks ago. I did some preliminary investigation into the House of Saud, Khalid in particular, since the vials were thought to have been sent to his palace. I learned the prince had an arranged marriage set up between his parents and their old friends. When I found out the bride-to-be was in London and liked to party, I made sure I showed up at the bars she frequented." Yasmin shrugged. "The rest was gaining her trust. The timing played in our favor. I thought we'd be the one to initiate the contact between Princess Aliya and Prince Khalid. But, the prince seems eager to meet his bride. When Khalid made known his desire to marry, we executed the plan. She fired two of the bodyguards, left with the third and I'm taking over her life with the prince."

Ben listened as Yasmin went through the steps she'd performed in a fairly short amount of time, amazed at how clever she was at collecting information and putting together a plan as complicated as the one they were about to undertake. "I hate to admit it, but I'm impressed. And you did it all in a matter of a couple of weeks. We sometimes spend months practicing an insurgency or extraction, down to making precise replicas of the buildings and rooms we will be entering."

"But, there are the times you go in not knowing who are the enemies and who are your friends. Right?" she asked.

He nodded.

"Then you go with your gut."

She was right. No matter how many times they practiced a certain maneuver, the situations were fluid and changed quickly. A flash of admiration filled his chest. Damn. The woman thought like SEAL.

Yasmin turned her back to him. "While you're in here, please unzip me. I need a shower before we fly to Riyadh tomorrow."

Ben stared at the fastener in the slinky red dress as if it were a snake.

She arched an eyebrow. "Seriously. I'm not going to bite you, and I don't want anything more than for you to unzip me. That zipper can be tricky."

Ben gripped the tab and pulled the tab down. Hell, it was long, traveling all the way down her back to the base of her spine and the uppermost curve of her bottom.

His pulse slammed through his veins the lower he went and the more of her smooth, dark skin peeked through the opening spreading wider across her back. When his fingers reached the bottom of the zipper, his knuckles skimmed the curve of her ass, and the tattoo of a brightly-colored bird that appeared to be consumed by flames.

A moan rose up his throat, and he swallowed hard to keep it from getting out. He pulled back his hand like he'd touched a hot iron.

"Thank you." Yasmin stepped away, clutching the front of the dress to her bosom. "I'm sorry, but you'll have to sleep on the sofa."

A shoulder lifted and dropped. "Slept on

worse."

"Soon as I'm done in the shower, you can have it." Yasmin nodded toward the door.

He grunted. "By the way, I like the phoenix tattoo." He kept his tone deadpan, while he fought to keep from smiling.

She frowned. "You weren't supposed to be looking."

He shrugged. "It's second nature for a SEAL to notice everything."

"Well, just pretend you never saw it."

"Sorry, that's not possible. Now that I know what's there, I can't unsee it, nor do I want to. The artist did a great job." He opened the door and winked. "But, he had an excellent canvas to work on." He ducked outside before the bar of soap she grabbed hit him in the head. The door closed in time for the soap to bounce off the wood panel.

With a chuckle, he crossed through the bedroom to the living area. After wandering around casually, pretending to study the layout of the apartment while actually looking for more hidden cameras or well-placed listening devices, Ben ended up standing in front of the huge windows.

The lights of London glowed brightly. From this location, he could see the Tower of London, the Tower Bridge, and the Big Ben clock on the north tower of the palace of Westminster. The River Thames reflected the city lights and the moon in its slow, steady path toward the sea.

Ben would have loved visiting the city on vacation, hitting all of the tourist stops to learn more about the history of London and England. He struggled with looking at the serene city without thinking about what would happen if a deadly virus or disease spread across the world. All of the beautiful architecture of past centuries wouldn't help keep the creators' descendants alive. The only way to stop the threat was to nip it in the bud. Contain the weapons before they could be unleashed.

"It's all yours," a voice said from across the room.

Ben turned to find Yasmin dressed in a sheer, pale coral baby-doll nightgown and matching robe. The garment left little to the imagination. A hard swallow did nothing to move air past the constriction in his throat. No amount of breathing exercises would loosen the tightening in his groin. Damned woman.

"What?" She rubbed her hand across her face. "Do I have something on my nose?"

"No. Not at all." He hurried past her, practically running through the bedroom to the bathroom beyond.

Yasmin's laughter followed him.

Ben slammed the door and turned to find candles lighting the room, filling the air with the scent of flowers. Holy hell, what was she trying to do? Ben went around to each of the flickering flames and snuffed them out with a quick puff of air. Then he stripped out of his clothing, stepped into the walk-in shower and turned on the cold water, letting it run over his heated skin. One minute went by. Then two. Five passed, and he was

41

still as hot as he'd been when he'd ducked beneath the spray. An image of Yasmin in that frilly nightgown had seared a permanent impression in his mind that refused to be washed away with cold water.

Working around Yasmin would be difficult. He found the woman simultaneously aggravating and tempting. Right now, he just wanted to wrap his hands around her neck and kiss the cussedness out of her.

He scrubbed his body and hair, giving up on chilling his desire. Besides, he couldn't stay in the bathroom all night. What if someone tried to get into the princess's apartment while he was in the shower? He wouldn't hear her scream. Ben spun, shut off the water and listened. Nothing made a sound. Was that because Yasmin was already dead, or was the insulation between the walls that good?

Suddenly anxious to check on the confounded agent, Ben grabbed the towel hanging over the top of the wall and quickly rubbed his body dry. Then he wrapped the towel around his waist and stepped out of the shower stall.

Yasmin stood in the bathroom with a thick white bathrobe draped over her arm.

"Do you always enter bathrooms when men are in the shower?"

"Only when they don't lock the door. I thought maybe it was an invitation." She winked. "I also thought you might like something besides trousers to sleep in." Yasmin held out the robe.

Damn, she looked entirely too sexy in the

nightgown. A growl escaped from deep in his throat. Already, his cock had jerked back to attention and was tenting his towel. He held up his hand. "No, thanks. I sleep in the nude."

Chapter Four

YASMIN CLUTCHED the bathrobe to her chest to cover the way her nipples puckered, making tiny little points stick out of the filmy fabric of Princess Aliya's nightgown. She deserved that. After putting herself on display in nothing more than the scrap of see-through fabric, she deserved to have Ben throw that little gem of personal info in her face.

I sleep in the nude.

Yasmin could barely breathe. His single comment had sucked the wind right out of her sails and left her dangling, living in anticipation of watching that towel fall off his narrow hips.

Holy hell!

Ben gathered his clothing and carried the items into the living room.

Yasmin trailed to the door of the bedroom. The question wasn't one of *wanting* to follow him. She *had* to follow. Her body had control, like a moth drawn to its death in the bright glow of a flame.

In the living area, he dropped his clothes on an end table, stood in front of the huge glass windows and stretched both arms above his head.

A slow anger started in her chest and moved upward in a wave of heat. The SEAL had to be putting on a show just to taunt her.

The heat of anger shot into desire as the towel slipped, caught for a brief moment and then fell to the floor.

Yasmin gasped, eyes widening. Her breath caught and held in her lungs.

His buttocks were tight, his thighs thickly muscled and his back rippled as he brought his arms back to his sides. Then he turned.

For a moment, time stood still. Yasmin's heart stopped and she couldn't think, speak, or utter even a squeak.

The man was perfect from the top of his head to the tip of his...

Then her heart started pumping hot, molten blood through her system. Heat shot through her body, pooling low in her belly, making her sex slick with longing.

Based on how thick and straight his cock stood out from his groin, he was just as excited.

For a long moment, they stared at each other.

Finally, reality set in, and Yasmin remembered the cameras in the corners. *Holy shit!*

She stepped back from the doorway into the bedroom. "You better hope my parents don't see you like that," she called out, though the sound was far wispier than she intended. "I won't have to fire you. They will." With that parting comment, she slammed the door and flung herself onto the bed.

The smooth satin comforter against her cheek and thighs wasn't helping. All she could think about was inviting that naked SEAL into the bedroom to slip his coarse hand along her cheek, down her neck and caress lower to the puckered tips of her nipples. He'd slide that big, gorgeous body between her legs and thrust his impressive cock inside her.

"Oh, sweet Jesus!" This was going to be the hardest assignment she'd worked to date.

Yasmin wasn't a virgin. She'd had a few partners, the last being the man who'd betrayed her trust and gotten her fired from INTERPOL. She had to remind herself she didn't need the complications of a lusty sex life. Not when she was playing the part of an Arabian princess on her way to meet her future husband. The last thing she needed was for Khalid to find her in bed with her bodyguard. In London, she might get away with such behavior. In Riyadh, she might be stoned to death.

Think stones.

Planting those two words in her head should have done the trick, but she could only think of how rock-solid Ben appeared. His muscles could have been carved out of granite. And his cock...sweet heaven.

Her pussy creamed, and she gripped the comforter to keep herself from running into the other room and begging Ben to take her now. Hard and fast. Again and again.

She slipped her hand beneath her nightgown and cupped a breast. What would Ben's hand feel like? Would he be tender? Would he squeeze her nipples? Maybe even bite them?

Yasmin moaned. As far as she knew, the bedroom didn't have cameras. She hadn't found listening devices, but that didn't mean they weren't there. At that moment, she didn't care. Getting out

46

of the flimsy nightgown became her top priority. Grabbing the hem, she yanked it up over her head and flung it across the room. So much for her plan to tease the big SEAL. She'd only managed to work herself into a frothing mass of lust. If she didn't take care of it herself, she wouldn't sleep a wink.

I can do this myself. I don't need a man to get off. She'd pleasured herself a number of times, usually with BOB, her battery-operated boyfriend. Tracing a line from the tip of one nipple to the other, she circled the tightly beaded tips several times, warming to the task. Then she trailed a finger down her torso to the mound of curls at the apex of her thighs.

Yasmin drew in a deep breath and glanced around the room, praying a camera wasn't recording her every move. She wouldn't mind if Ben were on the other side of the lens, watching as she dipped a finger into her wet channel and swirled until the digit was loaded with her juices, then she drew a line from her entrance to the little strip of heated flesh tucked between her folds.

"Ah, yes." She stroked once and drew in a sharp breath as the first tingle shot through her. Another moan rose up her throat, escaping into the cavernous room, proving to herself she didn't need a man to make her come. She could do this.

Again, she stroked, and more tingles rippled from her center outward. Yasmin twisted in the sheets, parting her legs wider. Closing her eyes, she imagined Ben lying between her legs, his tongue where her finger was, licking her in that place packed with highly sensitive nerves, begging to be

47

touched, nipped and sucked until she came apart into a million little pieces. Oh, God, if only Ben was there.

The door to the bedroom swung open with a bang. "Are you all right?" Ben stood in the doorway, dressed in his trousers and nothing else.

Caught in the throes of her self-induced passion, Yasmin stared, her eyes wide, her finger still pressed to her clit. "What are you doing in here?" she said, her voice shaky, her breathing ragged.

"I thought you might be hurt. I heard moaning…" His gaze swept over her naked body, zeroing in on the hand between her legs.

"So, now you know," she whispered. "I can do this myself."

He stood for a moment, his trousers pulling tightly over the ridge growing bigger by the second beneath his fly. Ben shot a glance around the room. His attention returned to her, and he took another step into the room. "Why do it yourself when you have me to help?"

Yasmin tried, but she couldn't manage to take a full breath as the SEAL crossed the room and stood at the end of the bed.

As if of its own accord, her finger stroked her clit and then slipped lower to dip into the dripping juices oozing from her channel. She'd imagined Ben between her legs, and there he was, larger than life, ruggedly handsome and one-hundred-percent male.

"Do you want my…help, or not?" He dragged a finger along the inside of her calf up to her knee. "I'm sure two can accomplish the task quicker than one."

"I like taking things slowly," she said, sliding her finger inside, adding another and circling. "A job worth doing shouldn't be rushed."

"You have a good point."

Oh, baby, and you have an even better point. Bring it closer. She willed him to stop staring and start moving as she drew up her knees, widening the spread of her legs. In effect, inviting him in.

Ben unbuttoned his trousers. Before dropping them, he dug into his back pocket, extracted his wallet, and removed a condom from inside.

Yasmin sent a silent prayer of thanks to the heavens for sending a man who could think with his pants down.

Ben hadn't come into the bedroom to make love to his partner on this operation. He'd come in expecting to find trouble. Hell, he'd found it in a big way. The naked woman on the bed with her hand on her sex had him tied in so many knots he could think of only one way to unravel all of them at once.

One step led to another until he found himself standing at the end of her bed, pulling a rubber out of his wallet. What the hell was he thinking?

The scent of her musk sent his pulse speeding through his veins. Her naked, trim body, with all that beautiful light brown skin and her wet entrance glistening in the light from the lamp on the nightstand, sealed the deal.

"Just so you know," she said. "I didn't ask for your help. I'm not expecting any future

49

commitment, other than what we agreed on to begin with."

Ben frowned. What the hell was she talking about? "I didn't offer to help with anything but the task at hand." He grabbed her ankles and tugged her toward the edge of the bed. "Now, shut up and let me assist." Code for *let me take over and make you come*.

He'd never been in a situation where he and his partner had to talk in riddles for fear of being bugged. The idea of someone listening in on their tryst didn't make him balk. The challenge made it even more titillating, and he dropped to his knees, draping her legs over his shoulders.

"Oh, my. Is that how…" she sucked in a breath as he slid his finger along her inner thigh. "Is that what they taught you in bodyguard school?" Yasmin clamped her lips shut and arched her back as he touched her entrance, slipping a finger inside her well-lubricated channel.

Her reaction to his touch fanned the flames burning inside. Ben parted her folds and pushed aside her finger, replacing it with the flick of his tongue.

Her heels dug into his back, her thighs closing on his ears. An image of the man she'd strangled flashed through his mind and disappeared. If he died due to strangulation with those incredibly tight thighs, he'd take her with him with what he knew would light her rocket fuel.

Ben tapped her clit once with the tip of his tongue, and then again. Next he swept it across, swirling, laving, and twirling the little nubbin of flesh while pressing his fingers into her entrance. He continued, slowly, steadily bringing her to the very edge until she writhed beneath him.

She weaved her hands into his hair, massaging his scalp with every thrust of his tongue and fingers. When her body tensed and she pulled hard on his hair, he knew she was almost there. One last tongue thrust sent her over the top. She rocked with her release, her breathing coming in short, ragged gasps.

Yasmin settled against the mattress, but she wasn't done. Her fingers on his hair tugged harder. "You're needed up here. Now."

"As you wish." His lips curled into a smile, the taste of her on his tongue. Ben rose to his feet, grabbed the foil package, tore it open with his teeth and rolled it over himself with one hand. Then he pressed his cock to her opening. "Do you still want my assistance?"

She tipped back her head, closing her eyes. "Oh, yes. Hurry."

He chuckled, looped his arms around her thighs and dipped the tip of his cock into her. "I thought you said all good things shouldn't be rushed."

"I lied." She grabbed his ass and pulled hard, thrusting him into her.

He obliged, taking it deep until he could go no farther. He held his position long enough to give her time to adjust to his girth, then he moved in and out, slowly at first. Carefully. Testing for noisy bedsprings. The bed was of the highest quality. Not a spring squeaked. It paid to be rich. The only sounds were the rustle of the satin duvet and their heavy breathing. She was tight, cloaking him like a fitted glove. And wet. Ben closed his eyes, letting all the sensations of being inside her wash over him. Then he was pumping in and out, slamming hard until he catapulted over the edge in an orgasm so complete he was left breathless and wonderfully in awe.

Several minutes passed before he realized he still held her thighs in his arms. He slid her up on the bed, moving with her. Then he rolled to his side, maintaining their intimate connection.

"Thank you for making that so much better than doing it all on my own."

"I aim to please. Consider me your faithful servant." He winked and kissed the tip of her nose.

Yasmin snuggled against him. "I chose my bodyguard well."

"Let's hope your parents chose your husband just as well," he said, slipping out of her.

When she reached for him, he took her hand and pressed a kiss to her open palm. "I'll go back to my couch. Let me know if you need further assistance." Ben entered the bathroom, peeled off the condom, dropped it down the toilet and flushed. After washing up, he left the bathroom, nearly walking into Yasmin.

She stood in front of him, her naked body flushed with lovemaking, her lips swollen and her eyes glazed. Leaning up on her toes, she touched his bare chest with her fingertips and kissed his lips. Then she handed him his trousers, ducked around him and closed the bathroom door between them.

For several minutes, Ben stood, wanting to follow her inside and make love to her all over again. But, that would be tempting the fates. Too long in the princess's bedroom would only be construed as what had actually occurred. Her parents would be flying home to straighten out their recalcitrant daughter, only to learn the real princess had flown the coop, leaving an imposter in her place. An imposter set on marrying the prince in Aliya's place.

Ben shoved his legs into his trousers, zipped and left the bedroom before he said to hell with the cameras and listening devices.

Yasmin, with her exotic beauty and passionate nature, was proving to be far too great a distraction than he'd first thought. Hell, she'd been a distraction as a blonde. In her natural dark coloring, she was even more beautiful and entirely too sexy for a covert operations partner.

For a long time, Ben stared out at the London skyline, willing his body to grow sleepy. After making love to Yasmin, he couldn't begin to rest. Sleep was so far from his mind he might as well stay up and do something else.

One hundred sit-ups later, he wasn't any closer to being tired. An equal number of pushups only made his arms ache. If he could, he'd go for a long run. But he couldn't leave Yasmin unprotected. As the fake princess set to marry a very rich prince, she would likely be a target for someone to take hostage. Hell, he'd fucked up by making love to her. He would never look at her the same way. Not after being inside her, with her legs wrapped around his waist.

Ben finally lay on the couch with his hands behind his head, convinced he wasn't the right man for this job. He'd ask Sting Ray to fill in as the number one bodyguard, if he couldn't keep his own act together. Risking the success of the mission wasn't an option.

Chapter **Five**

YASMIN LAY AWAKE past three in the morning before she fell into a disturbed sleep filled with cruel sheiks holding her prisoner, cloaked women throwing stones and one handsome SEAL fighting through a crowd of terrorists unable to reach her in time to save her from the rampaging women.

Waking with a start to the alarm clock buzzing on her nightstand, Yasmin stared at it, trying to remember where she was. A glance out the open windows revealed London, not yet awake in the gray light of predawn. One by one, the streetlights blinked out as the sun edged up on the horizon.

Today, she and her SEAL bodyguards would board Prince Khalid's private jet bound for Riyadh, where they would use whatever means at their disposal to locate the purchased vials of deadly virus.

For a moment, doubt swept over Yasmin. Was she making a big mistake? Was she overly confident in her ability to fool the prince into thinking she was a princess? Dragging the SEALs into this charade could land them in a whole lot of trouble. She threw back the covers and swung her legs over the side.

No. They couldn't execute this idiotic plan. It would get them all killed or imprisoned. She couldn't let the SEALs go through with this insanity. Yasmin ran to the bedroom door and flung it open.

"I can't do this," she said to an empty room.

"Ben?" she called out. No one answered. "Ben?" A strange, panicky feeling swept over her. He wouldn't have left her, would he? She ran through the room, checking behind furniture, as if he'd be hiding with the thought of jumping out to scare her.

Well, she *was* a little scared. Had someone sneaked in during the night and dragged him off while she'd slept through it all?

A hundred different scenarios ran through her mind, each worse than the last. When she thought her head might explode, she saw the doorknob turn, and the door swung open.

Ben entered, carrying a paper bag and two cups of what smelled like coffee. Balancing the items carefully, he kicked the door shut behind him and glanced up. "Oh, good. You're awake. The kitchen cabinets were empty, so I went out for coffee. I didn't know if you'd like it, but I picked up a cup of cappuccino for you from the shop on the corner. Black coffee for myself."

He was so casual and calm when she'd been about to come apart, worrying he'd been kidnapped, maimed or killed. She took several deep breaths and let them out before she could think or speak without screaming at him for leaving and scaring her half to death. "I love cappuccino," she said. "What's in the bag?"

"Scones."

Swallowing the incomprehensible fear she'd felt only moments before, she settled in a chair at the tiny dining table and wrapped her hands around the steaming cup of cappuccino. "Mmm, this is delicious."

"Glad you like it. I was afraid you'd want the coffee. I think of cappuccino as the sludge coffee becomes if you let it sit too long." He held up his cup. "I like my coffee straight, black and watery; not thick like old oil in an engine. It's almost a dying breed among coffee makers."

Yasmin let Ben talk about coffee like she really cared. It kept her from having to come up with something to say when all she could think of was wanting to strip the SEAL out of his clothes and take him back to bed. Which wasn't an option. Not with the cameras on them and an operation to launch.

Talking about what happened last night wasn't what she wanted, either. Coffee was a good topic. Safe, not controversial, and it didn't require a commitment they couldn't agree on. Not that one night in the sack was a reason to commit to anything. No.

Sleeping with Ben didn't mean anything more than scratching an incredibly satisfying itch. Once they found the vials, he'd go his way, and she'd go hers. They probably wouldn't see each other ever again. End of story. Why bring up the subject, if their time together was ending soon anyway?

Talking about last night was completely out of the question.

"About last night…" Ben glanced over the top of his coffee cup, meeting her gaze head-on. "We need to talk."

No! No! No! We don't! Yasmin broke away from his gaze and stared down into her cappuccino. What was wrong with this man? Men didn't talk about sex; they just did it. Most of them walked away without a second thought. *Wham, bam, thank you, ma'am. I'm out of here.*

"What about it?" she asked, refusing to look into Ben's blue eyes. Her breath caught and held, waiting for whatever he might say next.

"What happened didn't have to mean anything." He set his coffee on the table and leaned closer to whisper, "It was a mistake. I hope we can continue on without upsetting our arrangement. We should act like it never happened."

A mistake. A lead weight fell to the pit of Yasmin's belly. Why? This man was just a member of the team she'd have to work with to find biological weapons in a Saudi prince's palace. Ben meant nothing to her, other than a well-trained SEAL to cover her six. Then why did she feel like he had just kicked her in the gut?

She looked up, meeting his gaze, raising her chin. "You're right. Consider it forgotten." Then, for the cameras, she added, "Leaky faucets are never something to dwell on. Especially when they aren't handled properly. Besides, I'm meeting my future husband today. I have a lot to pack in order to be ready." With a tight smile, she pushed back her chair and rose from the table.

Without another word, she left the living room, walked straight through the bedroom and into the bathroom. Once she'd closed the door, she leaned against it, dragging in deep, steadying breaths. What was wrong with her? She acted as though she was in love with a man she'd only just met.

Her heart banged in her chest and her stomach bunched at the memory of the night before. Her reaction to Ben's lovemaking had to be a delayed euphoria from, granted, the best sex she'd had in...well, ever! That was it. She was disappointed he hadn't felt the same. Yasmin pushed away from the door and crossed to the shower, turned on the water and stripped out of the nightgown that had started as a way to shake the big SEAL and ended up shaking her instead. She shoved the gown into the waste bin and stepped into the shower.

After a thorough scrub to get the lingering scent of Ben off her skin, she dried and went to work on applying makeup like she'd seen Aliya do. The process took her longer and several attempts to get some things right.

Thirty minutes after she'd entered the bathroom, she faced herself in the mirror, satisfied she looked so much like Aliya the prince wouldn't have any doubt she was his fiancée. She'd applied thick black eyeliner, sweeping the line upward at the corners, adding luminescent eyeshadows in shades of gray and midnight blue. She'd contoured her face with foundation and several shades of blush to make her cheekbones appear higher. Mascara enhanced the length of her thick, dark lashes. And the final touch was a deep red, smudge-proof lipstick.

Yasmin had dried her dark hair and applied the

59

curling iron to the lengths. Then she'd pulled up the sides, securing them with diamond-studded combs. Her disguise halfway complete, she left the bathroom wrapped in a towel and walked into a solid wall of muscles.

Strong hands gripped her arms, steadying her. "Do you always take so long in the bathroom?"

"I'm meeting my fiancé for the first time. I want to look my best." She looked up into Ben's eyes, and butterflies erupted in her belly.

He backed her into the bathroom and turned on the shower, still holding one of her arms. "What I said before was your chance to escape any unwanted entanglements. From my side of things, last night was anything but a mistake. Making love to you was mind-blowingly incredible." He bent and claimed her lips in a kiss that stole her breath away. "Leaving you alone in that bed took every ounce of my self-control."

Ben released her arms, raised his hands to her neck and tipped back her head. Then he swept the length of her neck with kisses, dropping lower to skim across her collarbone.

He reached the edges of her towel.

As she waited, Yasmin couldn't catch her breath.

He didn't disappoint. With one decisive yank, he tore away her towel, leaving her standing naked on the cool tile floor.

Her nipples drew up into tight little knots, and she shivered in anticipation of what he would do next.

"You're beautiful without all the makeup," he whispered. He traced a line from her neck down to the swell of her breasts.

Yasmin drew in a sharp breath, her chest expanding, offering her breasts to him, to lick, fondle and suck. Hell, she didn't care. He could do anything, and she'd be helpless to stop him. Her knees wobbled, and her core ached with a need so great she thought she might explode if he touched her there.

Ben bent and pressed his lips to one of her nipples, flicking it with the tip of his tongue.

Yasmin moaned, clasped the back of his head and urged him to take more.

He did, sucking the entire areola into his mouth along with half of her breast.

Arching her back, Yasmin slid her calf up the back of Ben's leg, pressing her sex against his thick thigh. She wanted him. Inside her. Now. Fumbling for the button on his trousers, she flicked it through the hole and lowered his zipper. His cock sprang free into the palm of her hand.

She moaned. "Commando?"

He chuckled. "The only way to go."

Yasmin wrapped her hand around his thick, hard shaft and ran it down to the base, where she rolled his balls between her fingers. *Yes.* She'd thought about this all night long. "We don't have much time."

"How much time do we need?"

"Not much." She backed away, tugging his cock, urging him to follow. When her bottom touched the cool marble counter, she scooted up onto the surface, spread her legs and guided him to her entrance.

Ben touched her there, dipping in, but not far. He leaned close to her ear. "I don't have another condom."

"Fuck!"

His chest rumbled with laughter. "That's the idea."

"I don't care. Just pull out before…" She wrapped her legs around his waist, unable to think beyond what they were about to do. The operation, Prince Khalid, her hair and makeup and the other SEALs were so far from what was on her mind she couldn't remember why they were important.

Ben stepped closer, pressing his cock into her slick channel. "You feel so damned good."

"Ditto," she moaned, pressing her heels into his buttocks. Something about him being fully dressed and her completely naked made her even hotter. "Can you make it go any faster?"

"You're bossy."

"You talk too much." Reaching out, she grabbed his hips and slammed him into her. "Better."

Ben inhaled deeply and closed his eyes, his fingers digging into her hips. "Ready?"

"Way past ready," she said, willing him to go for it, fast and hard.

He pulled out so slowly, Yasmin wanted to scream. The move was an excruciating tease she couldn't stand.

Then he thrust into her, driving hard and fast, just like she'd wanted it. The slapping sound of their bodies coming together was just one more thing that shot her to the heavens. Waves of sensation washed over her, and she rode them to the end.

Ben thrust once more and held her hips tight, buried deep for several long breaths, and then he pulled out at the last moment, grabbed a towel and came into the soft terry cloth.

A sense of pure feminine satisfaction settled over Yasmin as she slipped off the cabinet, washed herself and wrapped a clean towel around her body. "Apology accepted." Flipping her hair over her shoulder, she walked out of the bathroom and dressed in a sleek white skirt suit, wrapped a soft black scarf around her head in the style of fashionable Muslim women and started to pack the clothes she'd need for her stay at the palace of Prince Khalid, her fake future husband.

All the while, she tracked Ben's movements out of the corner of her eye, her body still on fire from the fast and furious lovemaking in the bathroom.

At the very least, she now knew Ben wasn't immune to her. Though she'd promised not to get involved, she hadn't been able to resist the handsome SEAL. Hopefully, by the time the operation ended, she'd lose interest in him and be glad when they went their separate ways.

She shivered, not from the cool air in the room. The tremor was her body's reaction to her thought of growing tired of Ben. Fat chance. A lot more of what they'd done in the bathroom was needed to get bored with the man. Again, the fire inside sizzled, spreading from her core to her extremities. Well, damn. Being near Ben was a train wreck looking for a place to happen. Unfortunately, the disaster would probably happen all over her.

Ben paced the length of the living area, his fists clenched in knots, his cock still on the hard side from making love to Yasmin in the bathroom. What the hell was he thinking? The problem was that he wasn't thinking with his head. He'd been thinking with his dick.

A buzz on the intercom near the entryway jerked him out of his self-inflicted dressing down. "Princess Aliya, your car has arrived."

Yasmin stepped out of the bedroom, dressed in a white skirt suit and white stilettoes, with a black scarf wrapped around her hair and neck. She rolled a small suitcase beside her. Though the outfit was probably meant to be conservative and sophisticated, it was sexy as hell.

Ben swallowed hard and walked toward her. "Is that all you're taking?"

She laughed. "Hardly. I need a wardrobe fit for a queen." She tipped her head toward the bedroom. "The others are in there."

Ben slipped by her, inhaling the heady scent of her perfume, wishing they could stay in the flat and forget this insanely dangerous assignment.

His cell phone vibrated in his coat pocket, reminding him that he wasn't the only man going along on this little airplane ride. He wasn't even certain they'd be allowed on the jet. Thankfully, the three of them had been issued fake passports, and dossiers on their equally fake backgrounds, before they'd flown from Virginia to connect their CIA contact.

They had yet to meet with Princess Aliya's escorts from the house of Saud. The escorts might have orders to bring the princess alone. Ben's fists tightened. In which case, Yasmin wouldn't be going anywhere. They'd hustle her out of there so fast, the Saudis' heads would be spinning.

Though she'd said she could manage the mission on her own, Ben refused to let her go without backup. Whoever had purchased the vials had no great appreciation for the lives of others, and probably wouldn't hesitate to kill a woman masquerading as a princess. Since the CIA would disavow any knowledge of Yasmin, she'd be on her own. No one would question where she'd been taken or what had happened.

As a Navy SEAL, Ben knew his teammates wouldn't leave him behind. Even if he was killed, they'd do everything in their power to bring his body home.

Four matching suitcases stood in the middle of the bedroom. Ben shook his head. Yasmin was playing the part of a princess to perfection. He assumed no self-respecting member of a royal family would be without proper garments for any occasion that might arise. Grabbing two of the heavy cases, he carried them into the living area. He went back for the others and returned as the buzzer went off again.

"Ben, darling, would you be so good as to get the door?"

He liked it when she spoke with an English accent. Her dark eyes danced with humor as he passed. "Please stand away from the entrance." He waited until Yasmin moved out of view of the door before opening it.

The chauffeur, dressed in fancy livery, wheeled a cart through the entrance, collected all five cases and rolled them toward the door, where he paused. "Your transportation is waiting in front of the building," he said, dipping his head.

Ben started for the door.

Yasmin put out a hand and gave a slight shake of her head. "Thank you," she said to the bellman. "We'll be down momentarily." When the door closed behind the bellman and the cart full of luggage, Yasmin glanced at Ben.

"Is something the matter?" he asked.

"No. Nothing. Just a bit of cold feet. What if the prince doesn't approve of his bride? Our parents are living in the past with antiquated ways."

Ben nodded without responding, recognizing a prepared speech when he heard it. She was performing for whoever might be watching through the eyes of the cameras. He assumed Princess Aliya had expressed her dismay at being promised to a man she had never met. Having grown up in the United Kingdom, she had become accustomed to living like a westerner. Her English friends would consider marrying because of a promise between parents positively barbaric.

Yasmin drew in a deep breath, let it out and straightened her shoulders. "Well, standing here won't change anything. We might as well get on with it."

Ben opened the door and checked the hallway before standing back to allow the princess to walk across to the elevator.

She ran her card over the scanner, shot a glance his way and nodded. "Let's do this."

The ride down was so much swifter than the ride up the day before. As they exited the elevator, Ben's gaze scanned the building's lobby for potential threats. He was happy to see Sting Ray and Irish standing near the concierge, dressed in dark clothes and sunglasses. Unfortunately, Ben wore the clothes he'd arrived in the night before.

Sting Ray had a duffel bag and Irish hefted two more, one containing his own clothes, the other with Ben's.

The men nodded to each other, keeping talk to a minimum. As bodyguards, they would be expected to be seen and not heard unless absolutely necessary.

A chauffeur in dark livery stood by the door.

Yasmin dropped her key card on the registration counter. "Thank you for the lovely stay." Then she turned and crossed the lobby.

Ben stepped through the door first, checked left then right, searching for any apparent threats. Two large, dark-skinned men stood beside a limousine. Neither appeared to be armed. A black van was parked behind the limousine. Ben assumed the men, who looked like the Middle Eastern equivalent to bouncers, would be riding in the van. "Are you here for Princess Aliya?" he asked.

They nodded.

Only mildly convinced Yasmin was not in danger, Ben opened the door.

She stepped out into the dreary English air.

The chauffeur opened the back door to the limousine.

Ben took Yasmin's elbow, holding her back from getting in first. "Declan," he called out.

Irish dove into the vehicle.

"Now, you." Ben handed Yasmin into the limousine and slid onto the seat beside her. He glanced back at Sting Ray. "You can ride with the driver." He ignored the two dark-skinned man and nodded to the chauffeur.

The man closed the door, rounded the limousine to the front and got in.

Sting Ray slid into the passenger seat and the limousine took off.

Behind them, the two bouncers climbed into the van and followed.

The limousine crept through the streets of London until they emerged on the highway leading to a private airport where Prince Khalid's jet sat on the tarmac, probably fueled and ready to go.

Once they stepped onto that plane, there was no going back. They had to see that mission through to the very end. Whatever that end might be.

Chapter **Six**

YASMIN'S FEET HURT in the high heels. How Aliya walked in them, she had no idea. The straps bit into her skin and being pitched forward all the time made her feel off balance, or poised and ready to sprint. Thankfully, the limousine pulled up to the steps of the aircraft, and she didn't have to walk far to get on the jet.

Having Ben by her side made the whole ordeal that much easier to stomach. At the same time, she regretted getting him and his friends into this situation in the first place. These men were the heroes of their country. Taking them into an unsanctioned operation could jeopardize everything they'd worked for. Why the CIA had sent them in the first place, she could only guess. Perhaps, because they'd been in on the initial operation, unearthing the plot to use biological weapons against populations. She supposed that was enough of a reason to send them into the palace of a prince in the heart of Saudi Arabia. Nothing about this operation seemed easy. She hoped her disguise would be enough to get them inside. From there, they'd have to be clever enough to move around the interior of the palace undetected

At the bottom of the steps leading upward into the aircraft, a man in traditional Arab dress of a white robe with the red-and-white headpiece waited to greet her.

As she approached, the man dipped his head slightly. "Princess Aliya, I am Muhammad Rashad, Prince Khalid's trusted servant. It is my pleasure to escort you to his palace in Riyadh. Do you speak Arabic, or would you prefer English?"

His lip curled on one side in what Yasmin could only describe as a sneer. "My Arabic is quite rusty. I would prefer English, for now."

Muhammad again tilted his head. "As you wish." He waved his hand toward the steps. "Once you and your luggage are on board, we can proceed."

Before she could move forward, Muhammad stepped in front of her and climbed the steps.

Yasmin squashed her annoyance at the man's rudeness, telling herself he was a typical Saudi male, used to disregarding the comforts and needs of females. She would be hard-pressed to keep her temper in the male-dominant society. But, for the sake of the mission, she must. She cast a quick glance at Ben.

He nodded toward Irish, who sprinted up the stairs after Rashad.

When Irish reached the top, he ducked inside. In a few moments, he returned to the door and gave a thumbs-up signal.

Yasmin went next.

Ben followed close behind, leaving Sting Ray to bring up the rear.

Once they were all inside, the two security guards from the van joined them, pulling the stairs up and into the plane.

Khalid had spared no expense on the interior of the aircraft. The seats were covered in fine, butter-soft white leather. Tables were of highly polished mahogany, and all metal trimmings were gold. Yasmin would bet it wasn't just gold paint.

Rashad waved his hand to indicate she should take the chair opposite him. If she'd had much of a choice, she'd rather have sat with the SEAL team. Rashad would likely bore her to tears within minutes of takeoff.

Then again, she hadn't slept much the night before. Perhaps falling asleep in front of her escort wouldn't be a bad idea. A six-and-a-half-hour nap would leave her refreshed and ready to take on the entire House of Saud upon her arrival. Settling into the seat across from Rashad, Yasmin had the urge to pull her scarf over her face.

The plane's engines roared to life and the craft taxied to the end of the runway. A few moments later, they were flying southeast, on their way to their destiny.

Yasmin eased her grip on the arms of her seat, trying to relax. This would be one of her toughest assignments. Maintaining a cool, calm exterior would be an important part of keeping her true identity from being discovered. From here on out, she had to think, breathe and be Princess Aliya.

Rashad stared at her, his eyes narrowed.

Yasmin fought the urge to squirm. Rashad's glance made her feel as though he could see through her to the secrets she held close.

If he knew she wasn't the real princess, he didn't say so.

Instead, he leaned back in his chair. "Tell me, princess. How fares your father?"

"He and my mother are quite healthy and on their third trip around the world aboard their yacht. But, I'm certain you already know that." She cocked her brows and gave him a hard stare before lowering her gaze. Saudi women weren't supposed to be confrontational.

A fire burned inside her at the injustices of life as a female in a Saudi household. They got little respect, and the men could take on additional wives if the current one did not please him.

What if the husband didn't please the wife? Yasmin believed in gender equality. Unfortunately, women had few rights in Arab society. They weren't even allowed to drive. Of course, the men who made the rules swore they were for their own safety.

Yasmin called bullshit.

The typical Middle Eastern man could not be held accountable for his actions. If a beautiful, uncovered—meaning wearing no *abaya*—woman walked by him, he could not be tried for rape if he took her on the spot. Thus, the need for the woman to cover her body and face with long black fabric.

She wouldn't last long in this society. Her mouth would get her into more trouble here than it did back in the States. And she'd gotten into her share back there, having started a few barroom fights.

The men who'd come on to her hadn't

72

understood the words *back off*.

Yasmin smiled. They did now. One had suffered a broken nose. The other had gone to the hospital with a concussion. Hopefully, they'd learned their lessons, and they wouldn't pull that shit on other women.

"You do not resemble your father," Rashad announced.

Yasmin stiffened. She'd studied photographs of Aliya and her parents. Rashad's statement was spot on. "No, I don't. Many say I look more like my mother." She lifted her scarf and brought it up higher, covering her chin. Then she closed her eyes. "I find myself fatigued."

"The flight is long, princess. Please, make yourself comfortable."

Yasmin tilted back her chair and pretended to sleep. For at least an hour into the flight, her act was nothing more than a pretense, her mind going over everything she needed to do once they reached the palace. Finding the vials would be searching for a certain fish in an ocean full of sea-creatures. In this case, they'd have to find the man who'd purchased them in the first place.

As a female, Yasmin wouldn't be allowed to question men. And, as Americans, her bodyguards wouldn't be invited into the confidences of the Saudi royals. The task ahead seemed insurmountable. Why had she thought just getting into the palace would be enough?

Taking a mental step back and thinking through her courses of action, she knew the group would have to split up and search the entire building. Perhaps they could disguise themselves as members of the family to allow them to move around the palace more freely.

She wanted to snort. Like they'd let her out of their sights for a moment. She was the next wife of Prince Khalid. The man already had two wives. Why did he need another?

Hell, she knew why. Men had stronger needs than women. Why screw only one woman when you could have as many as you like?

What about the man who'd reported the transfer of the vials to Khalid's palace? Perhaps he had more information. Her boss had given her the name of an embedded informant who lived outside the palace but had connections within. Without her usual handler, Yasmin was flying blind. She wished she had someone feeding her the information she needed. Instead she had to rely on memory alone, rather than risk being caught with notes. If she could get out of the palace for a few hours, she might meet up with the man and see what other tidbits he had to pass on.

Between plotting a search of Khalid's palace and connecting with the informant, Yasmin felt only slightly better about the job ahead of her. The drone of the engines, and having her eyes closed for so long, worked against her. Before she realized it, her ears popped as the plane descended into Riyadh.

Yasmin sat up and blinked. Someone had placed a blanket over her and leaned her chair back. She swept off the blanket and laid it aside. Her scarf had shifted, sliding off her hair to pool around her shoulders. She unbuckled her seat belt and stood.

The seat Rashad had occupied when Yasmin fell asleep was now empty.

"Have a nice nap, your highness?"

Ben's deep, warm tones sent ripples of awareness across Yasmin's skin. She turned and smiled up into his eyes. "Yes, I did, thank you. Did you get any rest?"

"Didn't need any." He nodded toward Irish and Sting Ray. Both men had kicked back in their seats, each deeply asleep. "I stood the first watch."

"You mean the entire watch." Yasmin shook her head and glanced at the guards sitting at attention where they'd been throughout the flight. "Rashad?"

"He disappeared into the cockpit shortly after you fell asleep."

Yasmin leaned toward the window. "Are you sure we're flying over Saudi Arabia?"

Ben grinned. "We are."

The sound of the landing gear deploying made Yasmin's heart leap.

"Are you ready to face your fiancé?"

She nodded. "Now that I'm refreshed, I can face practically anything."

Ben looked out the window as the plane circled a private airport. "I hope so, because either they have some foreign dignitaries arriving soon, or they sent the welcoming committee to greet their new princess."

"Gird your loins and fasten your seatbelts."

Sting Ray blinked open his eyes and yawned. "We're about to land."

Yasmin took her seat, buckled her belt and tried not to think too far beyond the welcoming committee and fooling her prospective groom. One hurdle at a time.

Ben took his time making his way back to his seat. He would prefer to sit across from Yasmin and reassure her everything would be all right. But, how could he do that when he had qualms about their mission? In the middle of Saudi Arabia, they couldn't just run if the shit hit the fan. Surrounded by miles and miles of desert, they wouldn't get far before they died of dehydration, or were shot by the Saudi army or Bedouin tribes protecting their herds and families.

His gaze connected with his SEAL brothers. One by one, they nodded, each giving the other a silent acknowledgement that they had each other's backs. That little bit of encouragement calmed Ben. He could count on his teammates to have his six if they got into trouble. And they could count on him to come to their rescue.

The trick was to make this façade of being bodyguards appear real.

During the trip, Ben had remained awake, checking out the escorts the prince had sent along with the plane. As far as Ben could tell, they hadn't been armed while they were in London. Once on board, the guards had stepped through a door in the rear of the plane and returned with decided lumps beneath their white robes. As for Rashad, he hadn't appeared armed. That didn't make Ben trust him any more or less. The man had no respect for women, and he'd made it clear to his prince's prospective bride. He'd be one to watch.

When the plane came to a halt on the tarmac, the cockpit door opened, and Rashad came out. He glanced at the passengers but didn't say anything. Instead, he waited while one of the Arab guards lowered the stairs. When the man stood back and gave a slight bow, Rashad exited the aircraft.

So much for making certain his guest was ready to face her prince.

Ben's experience with the Saudi culture reminded him of differences in this part of the world, but he also knew Yasmin. Though her mother was from Turkey, she herself hadn't grown up in a land where women were dominated by men, where the men more or less owned them. She had to be stewing over Rashad's rudeness.

Rising from his chair, he turned toward Yasmin. She'd pulled the sheer black scarf over her thick hair, freshened her lipstick and slid on a pair of dark sunglasses. In her white suit and matching stilettoes, she was drop-dead gorgeous.

Ben's pulse quickened. For a brief moment, he had the sudden urge to block her path, to hijack the plane and take her back to London. This mission was far too dangerous. If they were caught, he and his men would be okay. But Yasmin...

She nodded. "I'm okay. Let's do this."

Reluctantly, Ben led the march to the exit,

walked down the stairs and waited at the bottom.

Yasmin stepped into the doorway of the aircraft and paused.

His chest swelling with pride for the woman posing for the cameras, Ben wished the circumstances were different. He'd take her away and make love to her until neither of them could stand up straight. For now, he held his tongue and clenched his fists, gaze scanning the crowd of Saudi dignitaries and royalty gathered to welcome Prince Khalid's new fiancée. For that matter, he hadn't expected the press to be there, snapping pictures of a female.

Yasmin descended the stairs one at a time, moving slowly, allowing the cameramen time to take all the pictures they wanted. She arrived at the bottom and several white-clad Saudis stepped forward.

"Princess Aliya," one of them spoke in Arabic, saying something to the extent of, "It is with great pleasure we welcome you home."

Ben had studied enough of the language to get by. He couldn't keep up in a heated conversation, but he could ask for directions and speak the equivalent of kindergarten Arabic.

Yasmin nodded and replied in Arabic, "Thank you." She glanced over the greeter's shoulder.

"Prince Khalid had matters of state to attend to, otherwise he would have been here to greet you." Her escort switched to English.

Rashad had disappeared. Her new escort led her to a waiting white SUV.

Yasmin stood outside the vehicle until Ben, Irish and Sting Ray were allowed to catch up. They performed the same routine with Irish ducking into the vehicle first, followed by Yasmin and Ben. Sting Ray started to get into the front seat, but another big guy had claimed shotgun. Sting Ray squeezed in beside Ben

The string of vehicles pulled out of the airport, lining up on the road.

Their driver followed a military jeep mounted with what appeared to be a .50 caliber machine gun, equipped with a gunner.

Ben sat in the back of the SUV, wishing he had his M4A1 with the SOPMOD upgrades. The weapon wouldn't be a match against the .50 cal, but he was a good shot, and it only took one well-placed bullet to kill a gunner.

Twenty minutes on the road brought them to a gated compound on the outskirts of Riyadh. Two guards manned the gate. Machine gunners perched in arched turrets on each end of the ten-foot high stucco fence inlaid with colorful tiles in an elaborate mosaic.

The deeper they went into Khalid's estate, the more Ben's gut knotted. Each additional level of gates and security made it that much harder for terrorists to get in…and spies to get out. He hoped they could find the vials they sought. Once they did, they'd be faced with an entirely different challenge to get them outside the gates.

Ben glanced at Yasmin, wanting to know more about this woman who'd walked bravely into a dangerous situation. He thought back to the attack in the bar and how she'd taken down a man and choked him senseless with nothing more than her wits and some incredibly strong thighs. Dressed as she was, she could easily pass for a princess. She held herself like one—her neck long and elegant, her chin raised high with the proud arrogance of a woman whose mere presence demanded reverence, even in a society where women garnered little respect.

Her gaze connected with his and she blinked, a hint of a smile curling her lips, letting him know she would be okay.

She was the one pretending to be a princess in a society that was known to be cruel to women who lied, cheated or otherwise broke the strict rules of their culture. Yet, she was giving him a reassuring smile. He wanted to draw her into his arms and kiss the bright red lipstick off her lips.

Too soon, the vehicle stopped in a sweeping drive in front of a massive building with arched porticos decorated in beautiful, intricate geometric mosaics of rich reds, azure blues and shining golds. Fountains spurted water into the air, and palm trees waved in a gentle breeze.

The chauffeur got out and walked around to open the door.

Sting Ray jumped out first.

Then Ben got out and held the door for Yasmin, resisting the urge to extend his hand to assist her. Men didn't touch women in public.

Yasmin exited the vehicle with sophisticated

grace befitting a potential princess and stood at the base of pink granite steps leading into the palace. A group of men gathered at the top, dressed in the traditional garb of Saudi royalty.

Ben recognized the white dress, or *thobe*, the men wore beneath black robes with the gold trim. Only the Arab royals dressed in the black and gold robes. Red-checkered scarves covered their heads with heavy black bands holding the fabric in place. The few women standing to the side wore black *abayas*, completely covering their bodies, with *hijabs* covering their heads.

The men seemed to be hovering around a central figure, a younger man, perhaps Ben's age, who stared at Yasmin with intense brown-black eyes.

Without being introduced, Ben could tell. He had to be Prince Khalid. Apparently, the man saw in Yasmin what Ben already knew. She was stunning, regal and deserving of the title princess. He hoped the prince didn't plan on moving the nuptials forward on the calendar. The way he stared at Yasmin, he looked like he would prefer to skip all the ceremonies and get right to the wedding night.

Ben's hands fisted. The prince would have to go through him to get to Yasmin.

Chapter **Seven**

AS SHE STARED at the gauntlet of Arabs standing at the top of the steps, Yasmin squelched the urge to run. One man in the middle caught her immediate attention. From the images she'd studied of the Saudi family, this had to be the young prince, the favored son of the current king. Online articles portrayed Prince Khalid as a charming rogue among the royals. Though he'd married twice, he was still considered one of the most eligible men in the Middle East. Certainly, he was one of the most handsome with dark, smoldering eyes and the deep shadow of a beard making him appear strong and even more masculine than his clean-shaven English counterparts.

Yasmin shivered. Though Khalid was most definitely a panty-dampening, beautiful man, he was just a pawn in her game to get into the palace and find those vials.

As she walked up the steps to the delegation gathered to greet her, Yasmin fought to keep from reaching out to Ben for support. He was the man who'd made her ache with desire.

Ben, light as Khalid was dark and taller than most men, climbed the steps beside her. He would tower over the prince and the other royal family members, if allowed to rise to the top step.

As Khalid came forward, Ben stopped short of the top, letting Yasmin approach the prince alone.

Her heart skipped a few beats and raced forward. This was her chance to convince the prince she was his future bride.

"Princess Aliya, it is with great pleasure I welcome you to my home." He spoke perfect English with a British accent, in a deep, smooth tone.

Yasmin remembered reading he'd attended Oxford, the same university where Aliya had studied several years later. She bowed her head. "Thank you, Prince Khalid."

"You must be fatigued from your flight. Please allow the women of the palace to show you to your quarters. They will give you details of the events scheduled over the next few days."

Again, she inclined her head and gave the man a subdued smile, hoping she was handling him correctly. Aliya hadn't gone into the details of meeting a Saudi prince's entire family. She had been in a hurry to get away before her parents discovered her deception and forced her to return home and marry a man she'd never met. Yasmin wondered, if Aliya had met Prince Khalid, whether she'd have changed her mind. Darkly handsome, he could easily have been a model on the cover of a magazine.

The group of black-clad women converged on Yasmin, grabbed her arms and led her toward the palace.

Ben started after her, but Khalid's men stopped him.

More concerned for Ben's safety than her own,

Yasmin halted long enough to call back over her shoulder. "I'll be all right."

The women led her into the palace through a broad, open courtyard and into a long hallway beautifully decorated with the geometric mosaics and palm trees. They passed through a large door guarded by two hulking men, each equipped with a ceremonial sword.

Once inside the room, the women released her and shed their *abayas*.

A younger woman swept the scarf from her head. "Please, we are free to dress as we wish in this part of the palace. No men are allowed inside."

Yasmin removed the scarf from her head and glanced around. She was surprised to find the room full of not only cushions, but couches as well. It was far more western than what she'd expected in a Saudi household. Dressing tables with mirrors lined one wall, and diaphanous curtains hung around the room like pale, colorful clouds. The women, devoid of their *abayas*, fluffed their hair and stood in front of Yasmin, inspecting her clothing, hair and makeup.

"So, you are Princess Aliya." A pretty young woman with long, straight dark hair hanging down her back stepped up to Yasmin. "We were wondering when you would come. There were rumors you were not pleased with your arranged marriage." She crossed her arms over her chest, brows arched, challenging Yasmin to dispute her words.

"Yes, I am here," Yasmin said in a smooth

tone, pushing the corners of her lips upward in a sublime smile. She turned to the older women standing nearby. "You know who I am. Please, I would like to know who all of you are."

"We are the members of Khalid's family." An older woman stepped forward, her chin held high. "I am Nahla, first wife of King Salman, Prince Khalid's mother."

Yasmin dipped her head in deference to the woman who would be the top of the pecking order in the women's quarters. "I am honored to meet you. I have read many great things about King Salman and Prince Khalid."

Her eyes narrowed but she extended her hands. "If you are to become my son's third wife, you need to know the first two. Fatimah and Erin."

Two women stepped forward, each wearing brightly dyed silk tunics and flowing pants.

"I am Princess Fatimah, Prince Khalid's first wife. Daughter of Prince Ahmed." She took a step back and the next woman came forward.

This woman wasn't what Yasmin expected.

"I'm Erin." She had pale skin, auburn hair and green eyes and spoke with a what sounded like a British accent. She held out her hand, western style, and Yasmin took it. "I'm not a princess. Prince Khalid and I met at Oxford. We ran into each other again a few years later, when we were attending a reunion of our classmates." She shrugged. "What can I say? I fell in love with him."

Interesting. Yasmin studied the woman. "Are you from England?"

She shook her head. "Dublin, Ireland."

"It's a pleasure to meet you," Yasmin said, a thousand questions racing through her mind. Erin had to be the palace's best-kept secret. She hadn't read anything about Erin in the research she'd done online.

Knowing it wasn't polite to ask personal questions upon a first meeting, Yasmin saved her inquiry for later. She met the rest of the women, trying to remember all the names of aunts, cousins, sisters and children, and failing miserably.

A servant brought a tray of tea and scones.

Gesturing toward the food, Erin grinned. "I introduced the family to the pleasure of English scones and tea. Now we have them all the time."

The talk was light, the women interested in fashion and celebrities, much like many women around the world.

Yasmin fielded questions and drank very sweet, hot tea until she could drink no more.

As the light through the windows dimmed, Nahla stood and clapped her hands. "Come, we must prepare for the evening meal."

"How can I help?"

"For now, you are our guest." Nahla waved her hand toward a hallway. "Here in the palace, it is customary for the men and women to eat in different rooms." She led the way into a large spa-like bathroom, sinks lining one wall, huge walk-in baths and showers on another side. Bath oil scents filled the air. All of the women washed their hands in the sinks.

Yasmin followed suit.

They touched up their makeup and brushed their hair before donning the black *abayas* they'd worn earlier.

A servant arrived beside Yasmin as she dried her hands on an Egyptian cotton towel. She held out a black *abaya* and smiled.

"Here, let me help," Erin offered.

Between the servant and Erin, they pulled the *abaya* over Yasmin's head and downward, covering her sleek white suit. Then they arranged the matching black scarf over her head and face until all that showed were her eyes.

Khalid's mother nodded her approval, the frown lifting.

The women filed out of their section of the palace, walked down the hallway and into a large room with a dining table at the center. Yasmin hadn't expected to see a table. Many Arabic families ate on the floor.

"Khalid is all for modernization," Erin whispered next to her.

Nahla sat at the head of the table, captured Yasmin's gaze and nodded to her right.

Clearly, the woman intended for her to sit there. She took the seat and waited for the others to sit. Erin sat beside her and Fatimah across. Servants set plates of food in front of them. She recognized some of the dishes as similar to meals her mother had prepared on many occasions. Others she didn't recognize, but she tasted them to be polite. The women were served course after course, until

Yasmin was certain her future family was trying to fatten her up for the kill. When dinner was over, they returned to their quarters.

A few moments later, a knock sounded. One of the ladies answered the door, turned to her and said, "Princess Aliya, you are being summoned."

Yasmin glanced at Nahla.

The older woman nodded.

Yasmin stepped into the wide hall, ready to follow the white-clad man.

"You are well, princess?" a rich, deep voice asked. Ben stepped out from behind the escort.

Her heart swelling, Yasmin clenched her fists, digging her fingernails into her palms to keep from throwing her arms around Ben's broad shoulders. She nodded and dipped her head, trying not to stare hungrily at the man. "I am."

The escort performed an about-face and walked away from the women's quarters.

Caught up in a rush of desire for the SEAL, Yasmin barely noticed until she glanced up and noticed that the escort was halfway down the hall. She hurried after him.

Ben fell in step beside her. "I asked special permission to tag along with the prince's escort."

"Thank you." She wanted to say so much more, but she didn't want to give them away. "The others?"

"Are well, fed and settled into guest quarters in the west wing."

Good to know, and typical. Women on one side of the palace, men on the other. No temptation.

"They tell me the prince's quarters are in the north tower and the south is the entrance where we all came in." Ben spoke quietly, like a tour guide stating the facts.

Yasmin's escort didn't speak a word, just kept walking and expecting her to keep up.

Finally, they arrived at a grand arched door. The escort knocked lightly and waited.

Another servant opened the door and swept his hand to the side, indicating Yasmin was to enter.

Ben started to follow, but the escort stepped in front of him.

"I guess this is my stop." Ben nodded toward her and stood to the side.

Yasmin entered the prince's private quarters. Here, the furniture and décor were more modern. Instead of cushions scattered across the floor, soft white leather sofas were arranged in intimate groupings. On one of them sat Prince Khalid, smoking a very English pipe, lacing the air with the pungent scent of tobacco. He stood when she entered the room.

"Please, come have a seat." Khalid waved away the servant. When the door closed, he sat forward. "You can remove the *abaya*. I do not require the women of the palace to wear them." He tipped his head. "However, when the entire family is visiting, we bow to tradition."

Yasmin slipped out of the *abaya* and smoothed her hands over the white linen suit. She glanced around the room, admiring the light and stylish decorations. "Your home is lovely," she said in her best English accent.

"Thank you. I had an American designer incorporate the most modern furnishings with a few of the traditional pieces." He waved toward the white sofas and black lacquer table. Against the wall was an intricately carved wooden chest with inlaid jewels.

"Your designer has very good taste."

"I agree. Would you care for tea?" He motioned toward the table upon which sat a tray with a very English teapot and cups. "I must say, I miss the tea from England." Khalid wrinkled his nose. "So much less sugar."

Yasmin sat beside him and poured a cup of tea, handing it to him before pouring for herself. She waited for him to speak first.

"The Saudi people have many customs that appear strange and constrictive to people of the West."

She nodded and sipped her tea.

"Some consider arranged marriages a thing of the past. A tradition that should have been buried with our ancestors."

Once more, Yasmin nodded her head. "And what do you think?"

"I would like to see my country shake off the old ways and become more modern." He sighed. "However, others who think as I do are few. Change does not come quickly; it must be introduced in small increments."

Yasmin could continue to pretend to be a submissive woman, speaking only when spoken to, but something in Khalid's statements made her take a chance. "If you believe the old ways should be retired, why consider our arranged marriage?"

He lifted his chin and stared into her eyes, his own unfathomable dark pools. "I am a man of honor. I respect my elders and what they have done for me. One day, I hope to assume the role of King of Saudi Arabia." He pressed a hand to his chest. "Then I will lead our country into the future." Khalid smiled. "Until then, I must bow to tradition. Our families arranged this marriage when we were small children. As a show of trust, I will go through with it, if you are still in agreement."

Yasmin stared across at a man who she'd come there prepared to dislike. A royal prince who could be plotting a biological terrorist attack using a virus that could decimate the human population. How could someone who seemed to want to bring his country out of the past and into the future harbor a terrible weapon within his palace? And why would he have married a foreigner like Erin when he already had a wife and expected to marry a third to fulfill a parental promise?

Somehow, Yasmin couldn't see the man sitting beside her as one who could unleash a biological weapon. But then, she hadn't seen a double agent in INTERPOL partner she thought she'd fallen in love with. She'd been fooled once.

"I admit, I wasn't sold on the idea. But, like you, I will do what must be done for the good of all." There. She hadn't committed to marrying him. She'd only told the truth. And truth was easier to

91

live with than a pack of lies.

Khalid set his teacup on the tray and stood. "Since we are in agreement, I will have the arrangements made."

Yasmin's pulse quickened. As she rose, she lowered her eyelids, hoping to appear somewhat submissive. "How soon can I expect the wedding to take place?"

"Within two weeks." He walked with her toward the door.

"Two weeks?" she squeaked. "That isn't much notice to plan a wedding and get to know your other wives before I become one of them."

Khalid stopped, a smile pulling at the corners of his mouth. "My other wives. So, you have met Fatimah and Erin?"

"I have."

He raised dark brows. "Do you have questions about them?"

"I might."

"Fatimah was my first arranged marriage. As you know, unlike most western cultures, Arab men are allowed multiple wives."

Yasmin nodded. "And Erin?"

Khalid's smile faded, and a faraway look came into his eyes. "The love of my life, and a woman with great patience." He glanced up at Yasmin and frowned. "Will this impact your decision?"

Yasmin shook her head. "I've only just met you. Love is not a factor in this agreement."

Khalid nodded. "Good. Then we have an understanding." He walked halfway to the door with her. "Is there anything else you need to make your stay here more comfortable?"

"I would like to visit Riyadh. My parents haven't brought me here since I was a small child. I would like to go shopping and get to know the area."

"I can have my chauffeur and bodyguards take you into the city."

"I would prefer my own bodyguards, if that would be all right."

The prince nodded. "As you please."

"Thank you."

"Rest assured, the wedding will take place soon, and then we can all get on with our lives." Khalid dipped his head and gestured toward the door. "May your dreams be pleasant." He turned and walked away.

Yasmin slipped the *abaya* over her head, adjusted the *hijab* and veil then stepped through the door. The two men who'd accompanied her waited on the other side.

Her escort led the way.

Ben fell in step beside her. "Well?" he whispered.

"The wedding is in two weeks." She glanced his direction, expecting a reaction of some kind, just not sure what.

Ben nodded thoughtfully. "I see."

She could almost hear the gears turning in his head. That gave them two weeks to find the vials and get the hell out of the Saudi prince's palace.

Facing forward again, Yasmin said, "I am

scheduling a shopping trip into Riyadh tomorrow. I expect you to accompany me."

Yasmin wanted to say so much more, to share her impressions of the prince and what he'd said about modernizing the country. More than anything, she just wanted to kiss the man next to her. The stress of pulling off a masquerade of this importance made her want some reassurance from someone. Once she entered the women's quarters, she'd be on her own again.

When they arrived at the doors, Yasmin faced Ben. "Later."

Their eyes met, and he mouthed the words, *I'll come for you.*

That night would be the first chance they had to search the palace. How they would do it, Yasmin wasn't quite certain. But they had to make the best use of their time inside the walls of Prince Khalid's palace. The sooner they found the vials, the sooner they could go home.

Which also meant the sooner she would go her way and Ben would go his.

A touch of sadness washed over Yasmin as she entered the women's wing of the palace. For a man she'd just met and made love to twice, Ben had made a permanent impression on her. One she'd find hard to erase.

Squaring her shoulders, she tossed off the *abaya* and went in search of her suitcases—one of which had a secret compartment where she'd stored a white *thobe* and red-checkered scarf like those worn by the Saudi men. Once the women were asleep, she

94

would do her best to sneak out and meet up with Ben. In the meantime, she would explore the east wing. After all, the informant had indicated the delivery had been made to the east side of the palace.

While the women were still awake, Yasmin made a show of familiarizing herself with their quarters.

Erin volunteered to show her around. Several hallways led off the huge living area. "Each wife has her own set of apartments, complete with beautifully furnished suites that include living rooms, small kitchens and several bedrooms." Erin opened one door to display a nursery. She smiled. "I hope someday to fill my apartment with children."

"Does Prince Khalid have any children yet?"

Erin shook her head. "I think that's why he's agreed to this arranged marriage. His first wife has yet to produce an heir. I think he's hoping you will be the one to give him a son."

"What about you?" Yasmin asked.

Erin shook her head. "Children of mine will not be in direct line for the throne. The child's parents must be royal descendants themselves."

Yasmin stopped and stared at Erin. "You were born and raised a westerner. How can you accept this?"

She gave Yasmin a sad kind of smile. "I do it because I love Khalid and he loves me. He offered to give up his life here to live with me in England. But, I know how much he loves his country and how much bringing it into this millennium means to him. If he is chosen as the next king, he has a shot at leading his people into a more modern world. I couldn't let him give up that dream for me. His people need him as much, if not more, than I do. So, I chose to follow him here."

For a moment, Yasmin had the urge to spill her guts to the woman, to let her know why she'd really come. But, it wouldn't be fair to ask Erin to keep a secret from the husband she loved so completely. Her loyalty lay with him, not the woman who'd come to potentially cause more heartache for her and the people she now called family.

Yasmin wondered what it felt like to love a man so much she would walk away from a familiar life and give up her freedom to be with him in such a different culture.

Erin laughed. "Don't worry about me. I made this choice and I've never regretted it."

For Erin's sake, Yasmin hoped she never would. If Khalid was the one who bought the biological weapons, he had the potential to annihilate entire populations.

Erin took her past Nahla and Fatimah's apartments without entering their quarters. "They will invite you in, when they get to know you better." Yasmin asked about other doors along hallways and Erin answered in her open, forthright way, seemingly happy to have another woman around who spoke English as well as she did.

"Nahla and Fatimah understand and speak English, but they prefer their native tongue," Erin said. "I have a tutor come in three times a week. I'm learning to speak Arabic, but I'm also learning to read and write in the language," she said with a smile. "When Khalid and I do have children, I want to help them with their studies and actually know what I'm doing."

Erin stopped halfway down the long hallway. "I'm sorry. I've talked so much I didn't take into account you might be exhausted from traveling today."

"I'm quite okay," Yasmin said.

"Still, we can save the rest of the tour until you've had time to rest." Erin turned back.

"What are the other rooms farther down the hall?"

"Oh, just storage closets and additional unused apartments. One of them will be yours to decorate as you like."

She didn't say it, but Yasmin filled in the rest. The other apartments could house additional wives, should there be any more than the two Khalid already had, and the one he thought he was getting.

Though Erin put on a game face, Yasmin suspected the woman would prefer to have her love all to herself. Or, Yasmin was imposing her own thoughts and beliefs on another person. If she were in the same situation, would she put up with other wives? All for love and country?

Chapter **Eight**

BEN SAT CROSS-LEGGED on a rug in the guest quarters he and his teammates had been assigned.

Sting Ray lay stretched out, his hands behind his head, his eyes closed, conserving energy for later that night.

Irish lounged on several cushions, sound asleep. He could be fully alert in seconds. The man had an uncanny way of recognizing danger.

Though they didn't have a guard outside their door, Ben had the feeling their presence was only tolerated in deference to Princess Aliya.

He didn't care, as long as he and his guys could slip out undetected later and search the palace. First, he wanted to get to Yasmin. He wasn't sure of the consequences of her venturing out on her own. Guards finding her alone might be better than finding her with Ben. Saudi custom insisted a female wasn't supposed to be alone with a male until she was married. Ben hoped hired bodyguards were excluded from the complications.

Time dragged by as the palace people settled in for the night. Soon, the hallway outside his room grew silent of passing footsteps. Ben wished he had a cellphone that worked. But then he'd be tempted to use it. The risk of a transmission being intercepted was too dangerous. When they made that trip into Riyadh, he'd purchase burner phones for Yasmin and each member of his team. Tucked into a secret pouch inside their duffel bags were radio headsets they could hide in their ears.

Ben crossed the room to his bag and fished out the radios.

"Is it that time?" Irish asked, jackknifing into a sitting position.

"Not quite. I wanted to check equipment to make sure we're ready when it's time."

Irish pushed to his feet and ran a hand through his shaggy hair. "I could use a gallon of coffee and a ham sandwich."

Ben chuckled. "You might find coffee, but the ham sandwich is out of the question. Saudis don't eat pork."

"What? No bacon, either?" Irish grinned and headed for his duffel bag. "Then I'll have to be satisfied with lamb, goat and chicken. Blah." He sighed and pulled out the tiny headset.

"Can't a guy get some sleep around here?" Sting Ray sat up and pulled his duffel bag close. He too, rummaged around for his headset before looping the nearly invisible device over his ear and pushing the bud inside. He glanced at Ben and Irish.

Ben settled his device in his ear and waited for Irish. Once they all had their radios in place, he turned his back, walked to the far corner of the room, and tapped his. "Comm check," he whispered.

"Sting Ray here."

"Irish here."

Ben swung around and glanced at his watch. They'd agreed to start their search at two o'clock in the morning, figuring most people would be asleep. Hopefully, the guards would be, as well.

They'd thought about finding traditional Arabic clothing, but that would have to wait until after their shopping trip in Riyadh the next day. In the meantime, their pre-arranged excuse for wandering the palace was that they were searching for the kitchen and a late snack.

Yasmin's excuse would be more of a challenge. Ben was almost certain a woman wandering around that late at night would be more than frowned upon. Yet, she'd insisted on helping them look through the palace. Ben should have contended she focus her search on the women's quarters. They weren't certain Prince Khalid had been the purchaser. He might have enemies among the women of the palace.

"It's almost two. We should begin," Ben said.

Sting Ray flexed his muscles and rolled the kinks out of his neck. "Any idea what exactly we're looking for?"

"Some kind of vials," Irish said.

"Something that looks like a dangerous plague." Sting Ray nodded. "Got it."

Unarmed and foreign in a royal palace, they already had a lot of strikes against them. But, they wouldn't find the biological weapons hanging back in their rooms.

Ben pushed open the door and peered out into the spacious hallway. So far, he hadn't seen signs of security cameras, but that didn't mean there weren't any. He figured they'd have one shot at playing the new-in-the-palace, looking-for-the-kitchen card. After they were caught once, they'd have to resort to Arab clothing disguises.

As he'd expected, the hallway was clear. He and his teammates stepped out into the corridor.

"Which way?" Irish asked.

"Spread out," Ben whispered. "We're likely to find what we're looking for in a lab, basement, storage room or office safe."

"So, all we have to do is open enough doors to find one of those." Irish shook his head and rubbed his belly. "I'm so hungry, I could search the entire palace for a slice of pizza about now." He winked.

"They fed us well," Sting Ray pointed out.

"Not pizza," Irish argued.

"Let's go, leprechaun," Sting Ray said. "Your *pizza* awaits."

"You know the drill," Ben said. "When we split, whoever finds pizza first speaks up."

"Got it. I'm betting the kitchen is in the basement." Sting Ray turned to the left at the first connecting corridor.

"I think I saw a door leading off the dining hall." Irish turned right.

Ben headed straight for the east wing. Because he'd been there earlier with Khalid's escort, he found it quickly. The door was closed, but the guard that had been there must have gone to bed. Ben reached for the door handle, just in case.

Locked. He tapped very lightly on the wooden panel and waited. He had no idea how big the east wing was, or how far back it went. He'd caught a glimpse of a living area when he'd escorted Yasmin to the east wing. The sleeping quarters had to be farther back.

After waiting a full minute, he knocked a little louder.

The door opened and a head poked out, covered in a red-checkered scarf with the black braided headband holding it in place.

Ben backed a step, wondering why a man was answering the door from inside the women's wing.

"Shh. You'll wake the others," a voice sounding suspiciously like Yasmin whispered.

She carefully checked the lock to make sure it would remain disengaged when she closed the door, before she stepped out in a long white *thobe* and the checkered head covering.

Ben chuckled softly. "Where did you get that?"

"Aliya's father left it at her apartment. I packed it for just such an occasion. I didn't think I would be allowed to wander around the palace in an *abaya*."

"Just keep your head down if we pass anyone."

"Believe me, I will." She grabbed his arm. "Come on, this is a huge place, we might need the full two weeks before my wedding to find what we're looking for."

"Pizza," he said.

"Pizza?"

"Code for our target acquisition. And, if we're caught, our excuse."

"You don't really think someone would believe you're looking for pizza, do you?"

He shrugged. "Or the Arabic equivalent."

They hurried down wide, tiled hallways.

"This place is massive. How will we ever find pizza here?" she asked after they'd tried several doors only to find them locked, or the rooms beyond to be empty.

"Just like eating an elephant."

Yasmin snorted. "One bite at a time." She pushed open a door to what appeared to be an office or study. Bookshelves lined the walls in deep red mahogany. A desk made out of the same rich wood took center stage, dominating the room. "Do you think someone would keep biological weapons in here? I would think they would be stored in some kind of refrigeration unit."

"If not here, there might be some evidence of where they might have hidden it. Who knows, there might be a safe behind a painting. We have to look." He pulled her into the room and closed the door. Once inside, Ben tugged her into his arms and kissed her hard. When he brought up his head, he sighed. "I've wanted to do that all day."

"Are you insane? We could be hauled off to some godforsaken jail for what we're doing, and you want to kiss me?" She shook her head, hooked her hands behind his neck and dragged him down for another kiss.

He searched for her hips, buried in the voluminous *thobe*. When he found them, he pressed her close to him, realizing it might have been a mistake. Having her close was good, but he wanted so much more. They didn't have time for making love, but he wanted to. And the potential of being caught only made their actions more enticing.

Footsteps in the hallway made Ben break off the kiss. "Did you hear that?"

"Yes." Yasmin grabbed his hand and dragged him toward French doors leading out into a garden. She pushed through. He followed and they ducked to either side of the glass as the door to the office opened and the light inside came on.

Ben eased to the edge of the glass and looked in.

A man, wearing traditional dress, entered, crossed to the desk and pulled open a drawer. He slid his hand inside, moved it around as if searching for something, and then withdrew his hand. The wall behind him parted between two bookshelves and slid open.

"I'll be damned," Ben muttered.

"What?"

"A secret room."

"Can you see inside?" Yasmin asked.

"No."

"Who's in the office?"

"I can't tell." Ben stared hard at the man. "He has his head down."

At that moment, the man brought up his head and looked toward the French doors.

Ben ducked out of sight, his pulse pounding.

Yasmin's eyes widened. She opened her mouth to say something.

Ben raised a finger to his lips and pointed toward the office. She flattened herself against the outside wall, merging with the shadows.

Ben did the same. He couldn't hear footsteps against the Persian carpet, but he sensed someone moving around the room. A minute passed. Ben started to lean toward the window.

At the exact moment, the handle wiggled and the door swung open. A red-checkered-scarf-covered head thrust out into the night.

Ben held his breath and remained perfectly still, his gaze capturing Yasmin's.

A noise sounded from inside the room.

The Arab ducked back inside and closed the French doors. A soft click followed.

He'd locked the door.

A sick feeling settled in Ben's belly. He waited several seconds before easing to the edge of the window. He was just in time to see the wall sliding back into place. Before it closed completely, Ben caught a glimpse of a white-robed figure moving about in the secret room. With the light still on in the study, they couldn't go back the way they'd come until the late-night visitor left.

By the light shining through the windows of the French door, Ben glanced around.

They were in a small garden. A path led to the outer wall of the compound where it ended in a T-junction. Ben forged ahead, turning to the left. The path led to another, then another, as if they were wandering in a maze of fragrant bushes. Finally, one led back to a doorway.

Ben twisted the handle, only to discover it was locked. He took out his handy pocketknife, unfolded a thin, sharp blade, and applied it to the lock.

"Have you ever picked a lock before?" Yasmin asked.

"Of course. Give me the benefit of the doubt. I'm trying."

"If it won't bruise your ego, let me have a whack at it."

He handed her the pocketknife and moved to the side.

As she worked the lock, he watched her by the light of the moon shining down from a clear sky, loving her take-charge personality and the sexy body hidden beneath the voluminous robe. "You know you're sexy in red-checkered headscarves, don't you?"

"Are you serious?" She frowned, her concentration on the lock as she wiggled the knife blade in the keyhole. "Here I am, trying to save our asses from being discovered, and you're flirting?"

Ben smiled. "You can never go wrong telling a woman she's pretty."

"There's something called timing." She jerked the knife and a click sounded inside the door handle. Yasmin twisted it, and the door swung several inches inward. She peeked inside and grinned. "I think we found your pizza. Only, it's not what we're looking for."

Ben's heart skipped a few beats at the smile on her face. God, she was beautiful. Even dressed as an Arab man. He swallowed hard. "What do you mean?"

"We found the kitchen. Well, the garden

entrance to the kitchen."

The radio crackled in his ear. "Sting Ray here."

Ben stiffened and cupped his hand over his ear. "Go ahead."

"I found the basement," he reported.

"And?" Irish piped in.

"A lot of locked doors. Should I attempt to open them?"

"Not now. The palace staff probably rises early. We'd better head back to our quarters. We'll check tomorrow."

"Aye, aye!" Sting Ray said. "Heading back to our bachelor pad."

"Sure could use a pizza," Irish lamented. "Heading back."

"I have a stop to make, then I'll be back as well," Ben promised.

"Give the princess a kiss for us, while you're at it." Sting Ray chuckled softly in Ben's ear.

Oh, he planned on kissing the princess again, but not for Sting Ray or Irish. He and Yasmin weren't nearly out of the woods, yet. They still had to find their way back to the east wing without getting caught.

Ben cupped the back of Yasmin's neck. "In case I don't get a chance to do this later..." He pulled her close and kissed her, his tongue darting between her teeth to sweep along the length of hers. The longer he kissed her, the harder for him to break it off. Time was running out before the palace staff began their early morning duties.

Yasmin cupped his cheek. "We need to go."

"Going." Ben kissed the tip of her nose, looked inside first and then entered the kitchen. He hurried past the bank of stoves and ovens and out into the dining area where he'd sat at a smaller table with members of the prince's bodyguard staff. He and his team had been allowed to eat with the security staff, in a room off the main dining hall. Not so close they could be seen or overhear conversations, but close enough to assist if the Arab royals needed them. Thankfully, he knew his way from that point. He waved for Yasmin to follow him. They made it all the way back to the east wing without running into anyone.

Outside the door to the women's quarters, Ben shot a look around, and then dared to steal yet another kiss before stepping away. "We'll shop tomorrow for more info."

She nodded, touched his arm and slipped through the door, closing it softly behind her.

Ben stood for a moment, wanting to go after her, but knowing it would be a really bad idea for a man enter the private quarters of the female members of the royal family.

Instead, he turned and hurried back to the room he shared with Sting Ray and Irish, a poor consolation to kissing Yasmin.

His brothers hadn't located the vials. But, they knew where to search next. The basement. Locked doors could be hiding storage facilities surrounded by concrete walls, perfect for containing dangerous biological weapons.

The secret door in the library? Ben shook his

head. Surely, whoever had purchased the virus wouldn't be stupid enough to store it that close to the royal family.

Unless they planned on using it against their relatives. The thought chilled Ben to the core. Yasmin was being considered for the position of third wife to a royal. Would she become a target? Maybe Khalid wasn't the one who purchased the weapon.

Perhaps they were looking for the wrong thing. Instead of searching for the vials, they should be searching for someone who had a reason to use them. A motive so great, they would consider annihilating a family, a city or an entire population.

Chapter **Nine**

YASMIN ENTERED the women's quarters quietly and hurried toward her assigned guest room, tiptoeing down hallways, praying she didn't run into anyone, especially while dressed as a man. She reached her door without incident, slipped inside and leaned against the solid wood paneling. With a sigh, she pushed the headdress and black band off her head.

"Please, tell me you aren't a spy sent here to hurt Khalid," said a voice from the shadows in the corner.

Yasmin spun in a crouched position, ready to take down the intruder.

A figure rose from a chair and moved into the moonlight streaming through a window.

Erin stood with her hands pressed to her chest, her eyes wide and worried. "Please, don't do anything to hurt my husband."

Yasmin threw the headpiece to the side and hurried toward the Irish woman. "Oh, Erin. I wouldn't hurt him. He could be my husband, too."

She shook her head. "You're not here to marry him, are you?" Her gaze traveled over the white dress-like *thobe*, and her brows descended. "Why *are* you here?"

"I really am not here to hurt Khalid." She reached for Erin's hands, desperate to get through to the woman, to keep her from running to the prince with news his latest fiancée was wandering the palace dressed as a man.

Erin stepped out of reach, her frown deepening. "You don't care about Khalid, his family or his culture. Otherwise, you wouldn't be dressed as you are. What were you doing?"

Yasmin struggled with the need to keep her secrets and the need to reassure Erin she wasn't out to bring down the House of Saud. She stared at the woman for a long time before saying, "Erin, I'm here to prevent something terrible from happening."

Erin pressed her hand to lips. "You *are* here to hurt my husband. If not him, then his family."

Shaking her head, Yasmin said, "No. I'm not. I need to find something that doesn't belong here. That doesn't belong anywhere. A danger that could potentially affect every human on the planet."

Erin stared at Yasmin. "What is it? What could be so dangerous?"

"Biological weapons tested on entire villages in Somalia. A disease or virus that, if released, could spread across the planet and kill everyone."

Erin's frown remained firmly in place. "Why would someone bring such a weapon into the palace?"

"I don't know. A recent raid destroyed the manufacturing facility in Africa, but intelligence reported a sale to a Saudi buyer. Someone connected to the palace."

Erin closed her eyes, her lips thinning into a flat line. "Women and children live here."

"Women and children were in those Somali villages. This weapon doesn't discriminate. I have to find it before it's deployed."

Erin opened her eyes again and stared hard at Yasmin. "You could be the one carrying such a weapon. You could be here to destroy my husband's family." She crossed her arms over her chest, lifting her chin in challenge. "I should turn you in, let Khalid sort through your lies."

Yasmin sighed. "I wish I was lying. I wish I didn't have to come here to find the vials of this horrible weapon. But, I'm not lying. I'm here to keep those vials from killing the men, women and children of this country, or any other."

Erin's eyes narrowed. "Why should I believe you? Are you even Princess Aliya?" Her eyes widened. "Oh, sweet Allah, you aren't," she whispered. Then she made a dash for the door.

Yasmin's heart leaped, and she grabbed the woman's wrist. "Erin, listen."

Erin struggled. "Let me go, or I'll scream."

Yasmin released her suddenly, but blocked her exit by standing in front of the door.

Erin staggered, regained her balance and glared at Yasmin. "You can't keep me in here forever. I'll get out sooner or later."

"I know." Yasmin drew in a deep breath and let it out. How could she convince Erin she was her side? "You can go out, tell the others I'm not who I said I was. I'll be either deported or thrown in prison, and someone in this palace will carry out his plot to exterminate whole communities, maybe even

112

entire continents of people." Yasmin stepped away from the door and waved toward it. "You do that, and all of the people in this palace, including your husband, are at risk. All of the people in the world are in danger. Would you condemn the babies in the nursery, your husband, your family, to die?"

"I need to talk to Khalid."

"Go ahead. If you do, he might take the matter to the rest of his family. We don't know who purchased the biological weapon, it could be one of them."

Erin's brows drew together. "You don't think Khalid bought it, do you?" She shook her head. "He would never do anything like that. He wants the world to know the real Saudi people, not the terrorists and zealots. Khalid loves his subjects and wants to move Saudi Arabia forward, not backward."

Erin obviously cared deeply for her husband and believed he only had the best interests of his country at heart.

Yasmin latched onto Khalid's desire to help his people. "Are there members of the royal family who don't agree with his way of thinking?"

"Of course, there are." Erin stared at the floor. "Many of the older princes are against any kind of change." She glanced up. "Do you think one of them might be the culprit?"

"Again, I don't know who bought the weapons, but I want to stop them from being used. That's why I was dressed as a man. I need to search the palace. I have to find it before the purchaser moves the vials, or worse."

Erin twisted the lapel of her robe and paced in front of the door. "I don't know whether to believe you or not."

Yasmin snorted. "I guess, if I were you, I'd have a hard time swallowing what I'm telling you. I'd probably want to go to my husband, too."

She nodded. "I want to talk to Khalid. Perhaps, if I told him I heard it as a rumor?"

"I don't think it matters where the information comes from. If the person who purchased the weapon thinks someone is on to them, we might not get to it soon enough to stop his plan."

"I'll tell him not to talk to anyone about the matter, but to check into it on his own."

"Again, he might alert the wrong person."

"I can't just go on your word. I have to do something." She threw her hands in the air. "These are my people, too. I love them." Her eyes filled with tears, and she covered her flat belly with her hands. "And...and...I think I might be pregnant."

Her heart squeezing hard in her chest, Yasmin closed the distance between herself and Erin. She engulfed her in a hug. "Oh, Erin. We have to find the vials. You and your baby deserve a long, happy life with your husband."

"And we need to find the bastard who would bring such a horrible thing into our home." She pressed her cheek against Yasmin's chest as sobs shook her body. "How could he?"

Yasmin smoothed Erin's hair. "Some don't have an appreciation for the lives of others. They only want power…at any cost."

"What should I do?

"I know it's a lot to ask, but could you give me the benefit of the doubt and let me continue searching?" She held up her hand. "I promise not to hurt your husband."

Erin pushed to arm's length. "You're very convincing."

Yasmin smiled. "I can be, when it's a matter of life or death."

Erin stared into her eyes. "You promise you won't hurt Khalid, or the women and children of his family?"

"I promise." Yasmin's pulse slowed a little, and she released the redhead. Hopefully, she'd gotten through to the Irish bride of the Arab prince. "I'm not here to hurt anyone."

The Irish woman's brows remained knitted. "Who are you working for? CIA, MI6, INTERPOL?"

"I'm working for every living person on this earth," Yasmin answered.

"Where is the real Princess Aliya?" Erin's eyes widened. "You didn't hurt her, did you?"

Yasmin smiled. "You needn't worry about her, or a third wife because she ran off, not at all interested in her parent's matchmaking."

Erin seemed to relax a little, but bit down on her bottom lip. "Okay, I won't say anything, yet." Her eyes narrowed again. "But, be aware…I'll be watching you. If I see anything that makes me think you aren't telling the absolute truth, I'll go right to

Khalid."

With a nod, Yasmin held out her hand. "Deal."

Erin shook her hand and turned toward the door. "Please, find what you're looking for quickly. I feel like we're sitting on a time bomb."

"In effect, that's what it is."

Erin turned back. "If I can help in any way, let me know."

"Keeping this," Yasmin tugged at the collar of the white *thobe*, "between the two of us will help tremendously."

Erin gave her a nod. "For now. But, if you are caught, I will disavow any knowledge of your activities."

"As you should."

The redhead left the room.

Yasmin eased the door closed and twisted the lock. Then she leaned against the panel, wondering if the woman was already on her way to her husband. Why should Erin believe her? Just because they spoke the same language didn't mean anything. As she well knew.

Quickly stripping out of the white robe, Yasmin folded it neatly and packed it and the headdress into the secret compartment of one of her suitcases. When she finally lay on the bed, she dropped into an exhausted sleep, troubled by nightmares. She woke in a panic several times.

Eventually, Yasmin fell into a deep, dreamless sleep and woke to a sound and the sun shining through the window.

Someone knocked on her door. She suspected

that was the sound that had drawn her out of her sleep and into the new day. Yasmin flung back the covers, stood and stretched. Then she wrapped a silk robe around her body and answered the door.

Nahla stood there, a tray loaded with tea things and a plate of scones balanced in one hand, her other hand fisted to knock again. In Arabic, the older woman said good morning.

Yasmin responded, also in Arabic.

Nahla continue to speak in her native tongue.

Though Yasmin understood, she held up her hand, pretending she didn't. Understanding the language was one of Yasmin's secret weapons. "I only know a few words. But, I'm sure I'll learn quickly." She held out her hands. "Please, let me hold that. It must be heavy."

Nahla allowed her to take the tray and carry it to a low table in the sitting area of her room. "Your escort into Riyadh will be ready in thirty minutes." She backed toward the door.

"Thank you." Yasmin's brows twisted, and she smiled gently. Nahla's face appeared lined with wisdom. If she only had more time, Yasmin was sure she'd learn a lot from the older woman. "Won't you stay and have tea with me?"

Nahla shook her head. "I must attend to things."

Yasmin nodded. "Thank you for the tea."

Nahla backed out of the room and closed the door.

If Yasmin truly was the prospective bride of Nahla's son, she would have insisted on breaking bread with her future mother-in-law. The sooner the mother of the groom accepted the bride, the happier the entire family would be.

Frankly, Yasmin was glad the woman didn't stay for tea. At least she didn't have to rush her out the door in order to be ready by the time her escort came.

Thirty minutes later, dressed in the black *abaya* Nahla had given her the day before, Yasmin waited by the door for her escort, her pulse picking up at the thought of all she needed to accomplish while in Riyadh. She hoped she wouldn't have to keep the palace escort close at hand.

A knock sounded. Yasmin opened the door to a palace guard, dressed in the white robe and red-checkered scarf. Her gaze only briefly skimmed the guard and then shifted to the man standing beside him.

Ben nodded, the corners of his mouth twitching as if he held back a smile.

Yasmin was glad for the veil over her face that hid the answering grin. Just seeing him standing there made her heart flutter. She wanted to ask where the other two SEALs were, but she held her tongue as they passed through the hallways and out a side entrance of the palace. A large white SUV parked near the doorway. Sting Ray and Irish stood beside it.

As Yasmin approached, Sting Ray opened the rear door.

Yasmin gathered the fabric of her *abaya* and slid into the SUV. She didn't like how the outfit limited her vision, making it hazy, decreasing her peripheral acuity. She *did* like the anonymity it gave her. She could be any other woman on the street, escorted by her man.

The three SEALs climbed into the back of the SUV with her, the escort slid into the front passenger seat and the driver drove through the gates onto the highway.

Within twenty minutes, they had entered Riyadh and were navigating the narrow streets near the center of the old part of the city, as she'd requested, saying she wanted to experience traditional shopping, not the specialty or superstore experiences.

When the vehicle could get no closer to the busy market, the driver pulled to the curb and got out.

Ben exited the vehicle, rounded to the driver's door and spoke to the chauffeur. He returned to hold the door for Yasmin. "I instructed the driver to leave us here and wait until you'd completed your shopping."

Yasmin leaned closer to Ben and whispered, "Any chance of losing our escort?"

"I hope so."

"Phone first?" she asked.

Ben nodded. "The guys are splitting from us in search of the shop we need." He tapped his ear. "We can communicate."

They entered the marketplace filled with every kind of shop Yasmin could imagine, selling everything from Persian rugs to strange and familiar

119

produce. She pretended to admire a rug for several minutes and then moved on to a shop with tunics, hijabs and pashmina scarves. The escort stood with his back to her and the shop in what Yasmin could only assume was his way of respecting her privacy.

Ben leaned his head around the corner of the shop. "There's an alley," he whispered. While the escort had his back turned, Ben ducked down the alley.

Yasmin followed.

On the next street, Ben weaved in and out of the crowd, putting distance between them and Khalid's escort.

Yasmin glanced over her shoulder. "Go into the hookah shop. Our escort just made it to the corner, but he hasn't spotted us yet."

Ben entered the hookah shop, and Yasmin follow a couple steps behind, her head lowered in deference to her escort.

The male shop owner scowled at Yasmin and said something in rapid-fire Arabic.

With her rudimentary grasp of the language, Yasmin couldn't make heads or tails of the man's angry tirade.

"What's he saying?" Ben asked.

"I don't know for sure, but I think he's telling me to get out and come back with my husband."

Ben shot the man a quelling glance. He still wore the shirt and trousers of a westerner. "You're with me." He grabbed her arm and pulled her close to his side.

The shopkeeper's glare deepened, but he

stopped yelling at Yasmin.

She moved around the store, pretending to inspect the hookah pipes in the window, giving her the opportunity to look outside.

Ben stopped beside her. "And?"

"Two stores down, heading this way," she whispered.

"There's a phone store a few doors away. As soon as our escort gives up and goes back to the car, we can head over."

The big Arab scowled as he neared the hookah shop.

Ben pulled Yasmin behind a shelf full of smoking and pipe paraphernalia. His hand on hers shot electric currents up her arm and throughout her body. Out of sight of the shopkeeper and the front door, Ben stared down into Yasmin's eyes for a long moment. "How is it you make me hot when all I can see is your eyes?"

The shopkeeper yelled something.

"I think he wants us out of his shop," Yasmin said, unable to pull her gaze from Ben's clear blue eyes.

"I'll see if we've lost our tail," Ben said, without moving.

Again, the shopkeeper yelled.

Ben shook his head, breaking eye contact. He stepped around the shelf and wandered around the items in the store toward the window.

Her heart thumping hard against her ribs, Yasmin stood where she could see Ben. The man had her tied in knots and didn't know it. Which probably was a good thing. They were nowhere near suited for each other. Well, maybe for a brief fling, but nothing more. Two people in highly dangerous professions, separated by distance and busy schedules could never make a relationship work. Not that she was thinking of a relationship with Ben. No. That would be foolish. Stupid. Insane.

She sighed. A dream that would never come true.

"He's gone," Ben said softly and moved toward the exit.

Yasmin hurried after him.

Ben glanced in both directions before he stepped out and crossed to the phone store.

Yasmin followed.

The shop owner was younger and more tolerant, allowing Yasmin to accompany Ben.

Inside, he selected a couple burner phones, tapped the headset in his ear and reported to Sting Ray and Irish. "Found phones."

Yasmin listened unashamedly to the one-sided conversation.

"Good. Get two and we will, too," Ben said. "We'll swap numbers as soon as we get them up and running." He ended the call, paid for the devices with cash and took the mobile phones out of their packages. They left the store and found a deserted alley. Within a few minutes, he had both on and passed the numbers to Sting Ray and Irish.

As soon as Yasmin had hers in hand, she entered the number for her supervisor and handler, Joe Spaneth, back in the States.

Joe answered in a groggy tone, "I thought you were going to stay off the grid. Do you know what time it is?"

"Need to know how to get in touch with your contact in Riyadh," she said, her voice low and intense.

Joe yawned in her ear. "I'm not sure he *wants* to be contacted."

"I don't care. I need to know exactly what he knows. The sooner the better."

"What's going on?" Joe asked, his voice sounding more alert.

"It's best if I don't fill you in. If you're questioned, you can honestly say you knew nothing."

"Evans, it's too early in the morning for doubletalk. Just a minute." The line went quiet for a full minute before Joe came back on. "I checked. He said he'd take your call." He gave them the number. "He sounded nervous. When you call, tell him Joe sent you. I take it you're in Riyadh?"

"You don't know anything," Yasmin repeated.

"You're right," Joe sighed. "I don't know anything."

Yasmin ended the call, punched the numbers Joe had given her and waited.

Ben stood at the end of the alley, keeping watch.

A man answered in Arabic.

"Joe sent me," she said.

"Where are you now?"

"In the old marketplace in Riyadh."

Dead silence met her announcement.

"Find the carpet market. Look for the store with the brass gong hanging in front. Be there in ten minutes. You'd better hurry. If I get there before you, I won't wait."

"Understood," Yasmin agreed.

The call ended abruptly.

Yasmin glanced across at Ben. "We have exactly ten minutes to find the carpet market and get the stall with the brass gong before the contact does, or he leaves."

Ben hit the redial button on his cell phone. "Be at the carpet market in ten minutes. I don't know, but find it. And be there on time. The ten minutes is non-negotiable. Earlier, if you can make it." He ended the call and pocketed his phone. "Ready?"

When she'd put in the call to speak with Joe's contact, she hadn't expected to meet with him so quickly, but she'd learned an agent had to take the opportunities when they presented themselves. If the guy had information that would help them find the vials of death, they had to find the time and place. "Let's go."

Chapter **Ten**

THE BURNER PHONES were bottom of the line and cheap, unable to give them precise directions from where they stood to the carpet market. They would have to get there the old-fashioned way.

By asking for directions.

Ben hurried out of the alley and asked the first vendor he came to where he could find the carpet market.

The vendor gave him a quizzical glance and waved at the carpets hanging in his store.

Shaking his head, Ben moved to the next vendor, wishing he had a good quality smartphone with a map application.

At the next vendor, Ben tried again. His Arabic wasn't the best. He'd had some training in Arabic when he'd been sent on missions to Iraq years ago. He'd had a crash course in Pashto before he'd deployed to Afghanistan. Unfortunately, he hadn't used Arabic in a couple years. He could barely say hello and where's the bathroom.

The shop owner frowned and spoke in Arabic.

"Do you speak English?" Ben asked.

The man shook his head and pointed to the Persian carpets hanging on his walls.

"We don't have time for this." Yasmin backed out of the vendor's shop.

Ben moved to the next, and the next, until they found a young man who spoke English, who gave them directions. The distance would make it difficult for them to reach the carpet market on time. Ben could jog there with time to spare, but that would draw attention and leaving Yasmin behind was not an option. They had to get there on foot, walking as fast as they could through the crowded market.

Ben took off, weaving sharply between people, vegetable stands and scarf salesmen. Several times he glanced back, worried Yasmin, dressed in the black *abaya*, wouldn't be able to keep up.

But, she managed to stay practically on his heels. The woman was remarkable. By the time they reached the edge of the carpet market, nine and a half minutes had passed. "Now what?" Ben asked.

"The vendor with the brass gong," Yasmin reminded him. "Find him."

Ben led the way down the long aisle between carpet salesmen. Every vendor made a plea to buy his carpets. Shaking his head, Ben pushed through. Even if he had a need for a carpet, he didn't have time to stop and view the hundreds of varieties of Persian rugs.

Almost to the end of the gauntlet of carpet salesmen, he spotted a gong the size of a trashcan lid hanging in front of one of the carpet stores.

A little old man sat cross-legged on the floor.

As Ben and Yasmin approached, he rocked and sang in Arabic.

"Excuse me, sir," Ben tried to interrupt.

The old man rocked more violently and grew louder.

Afraid the wrong people would discover them, Ben backed away from the little man. "There's not another gong, is there?"

Yasmin touched his arm. "Ben, over here." He glanced over his shoulder. She had a tight hold on his sleeve and tugged him toward the carpet store on the opposite side of the narrow street.

A man peered out from between hanging rugs. He waved at Ben without speaking. Though he had dark hair and dark eyes, his skin was light and he didn't have the typical features of an Arab.

Yasmin slipped between the rugs and disappeared.

A stab of fear pushed him forward. He shot a glance toward either end of the narrow street. Sting Ray and Irish had yet to arrive. They had his cell phone number. When they got closer, they'd either call or use their radio headsets. Ben pushed aside the rugs and entered a small office area.

A man stood in the office with Yasmin. He had dark circles beneath his eyes, and his hand shook as he pushed it through his hair.

"Ben, this is Omar. For the record, it's not his real name, but it's enough. Omar, Ben," Yasmin said, by way of introduction.

Omar nodded without attempting to shake hands. "Why are you here?"

"We've come to follow up on your report about a certain delivery to the palace," Yasmin said.

Omar dropped to sit on the end of a pile of rugs and buried his head in his hands. "Ever since I got word from my contact at the palace about the delivery of that box from the Ethiopian pharmacy, I've been followed. I didn't notice at first. Then, while I was at work one day, someone broke into my apartment. They didn't take anything, but things that had been on the counter had been moved. I haven't been back to my apartment in days. I'm afraid to sleep for fear whoever is following me will catch up while my eyes are closed."

"Has anyone actually attacked you?" Yasmin asked.

Omar shook his head. "Not me. But, the man who told me about the delivery had his throat slit in his sleep a week ago."

Yasmin stepped closer. "What more can you tell us about the delivery?"

Omar stared down at his hands. "Not much. Just that my contact wasn't allowed to touch it. He was told to leave the east delivery dock until the item was moved."

Ben wasn't sure they had any more information than before, and he was getting impatient to conclude the meeting and get back to searching the palace. "Who came to collect it?"

"My contact didn't know, since they made him leave."

"This isn't helping," Ben grumbled.

Yasmin's eyes flashed. She dropped the veil from the lower half of her face. "Omar. We believe whatever is in that box could cause serious and irreparable harm to the people of the palace and every person in Riyadh, including you. Is there anyone living among the royal family who'd want to harm a lot of people?"

Omar's gaze darted to the back of the small shop.

Out front, in the narrow street, the little old man with the gong started singing again. His voice sounded like a musical moan, getting louder.

"Someone's out front," Omar said.

"I'm expecting my men." Ben crossed to the two hanging rugs and parted them barely enough to see out.

Instead of Sting Ray and Irish, a couple of men wearing white robes stood at the gong across the way, carrying AK47s. They poked at the old man.

He wailed louder.

"We need to leave," Ben said. "Now." He grabbed Yasmin's hand and dragged her toward the back door.

Omar followed.

"Omar, anything you know might be key to our investigation," Yasmin whispered as she passed in front of him. "Any family discord? Any cousins jostling for power? Disgruntled employees?"

"Not all of the royal family is happy with Prince Khalid's direction and push to modernize the country," Omar said. "I heard the king has picked Khalid as his successor, rather than the next eldest crown prince."

"Who is dissatisfied?" Yasmin insisted, even as she slipped through the back door.

"Who is next eldest?" Ben asked.

"Prince Bandar, the defense minister, is particularly unhappy with the policies the king has adopted based on Prince Khalid's recommendation. Prince Bandar is next eldest of the crown princes and should take over if something happens to the king."

The old man across the street was practically screaming. Suddenly, he went silent.

Ben's chest tightened.

"Do you think, they hurt the old man?" Yasmin clamped her lips tight and balled her hands into fists. "Bastards." She started back through the door into the carpet shop.

Ben grabbed her arm and dragged her backward as the carpets parted and the two men brandishing AK47s peered through. "Time to go." Ben yanked Yasmin through the door and slammed it shut. He figured they had less than two seconds to make it to the next alley before the goons with the guns burst through the door and started shooting.

Yasmin and Ben caught up with Omar just as the man tripped, landing on his hands and knees.

Ben shoved Yasmin. "Run!" He slowed to scoop a hand beneath Omar's elbow and hefted the man to his feet.

The door behind them slammed open, and the two men with the AK47s jettisoned through.

Two feet. Two lousy feet to the corner. That's all they needed to get out of weapon range. Ben pushed forward, lugging Omar.

The gunmen opened fire.

Crying out, Omar jerked and fell to the ground.

Ben dove for the corner, slipped around and stopped.

"What are you waiting for?" Yasmin tried to grab his arm and pull him away.

"We won't make it to the next street," Ben said. He bunched his fists and waited.

Footsteps sounded in the loose gravel as the attackers ran toward them.

When they rounded the corner, Ben was ready. He slammed his hands on their weapons.

One of the men fired off a round, hitting himself in the foot. He screamed, threw down his weapon and grabbed for his foot.

Before the other guy could lift his rifle, Ben swung his elbow, clipped the guy in the nose and sent him flying up against a wall. His head hit with a dull thud, and he slid down the wall, unconscious.

The guy who'd shot himself let go of his injured foot and lunged for Ben.

Yasmin appeared like a dark ghost, flying in beside him. She hiked up her *abaya* and landed a kick in the side of the attacker's head, sending him down for the count.

"I'll deal with these two," Ben said. "Check on Omar."

Ben used his belt to secure one of the attacker's wrists behind his back. He used the other man's headscarf to bind him. While tying the man's wrists, Ben found a .45 caliber handgun tucked beneath his *thobe*. He shoved the gun into his waistband and covered it with his shirt, leaving the tail hanging out of his pants. Then he turned to Yasmin as she leaned over Omar.

The man stared up at her, blood trickling out of

the corner of his mouth, a stain spreading across his white robe.

"Omar, hang in there. We'll get an ambulance to take you to the hospital," Yasmin said.

The man on the ground grabbed her hand and held on. "Rumor," he said, his voice raspy, bubbling with the blood.

"What rumor?" Yasmin asked.

"Someone in royal family…funding…ISIS."

Ben had to lean closer to hear the last words spoken by the brave informant. When he heard the name of the band of murdering terrorists, he stilled, his heart sinking into the pit of his belly.

They were all doomed if the biological weapons made it into the hands of ISIS.

Yasmin felt for a pulse.

Omar had taken a bullet through the back, into his chest. The chances he would survive were minimal, but she couldn't leave him to die alone. She pressed her fingers to the base of his throat and held her breath. Shifting her hand, she tried again.

Ben brushed aside her hand and felt for himself. "He's dead."

Yasmin knew but didn't want it to be true. Omar had risked his life to meet with them, and he'd died for it. Guilt rose to clog her throat, and angry tears stung her eyes.

Ben hooked Yasmin's arm and urged her to her feet. "We have to get out of here. The gunfire will bring police and others. The sooner we're away, the better."

Yasmin nodded and moved away from the dead man and the attackers, securing the veil over her nose and mouth.

"My knot-tying won't keep those goons down long." Ben headed toward the narrow street through the busy carpet market.

Knowing she couldn't help Omar, Yasmin followed.

As Yasmin emerged near the carpet stall with the gong, she saw the old man, lying in a bloody heap among his carpets. Her chest squeezed tightly. She straightened her shoulders and pushed on. She didn't have time to let herself feel any more deeply. They had to get out of there before the two men who'd attacked them were found and released.

Sting Ray and Irish appeared, running toward them.

"We heard gunfire," Irish said, slowing to stop in front of them.

"You heard right," Ben said. "We need to leave. Now." He turned left and hurried down the long line of carpet sellers.

Yasmin matched Ben, stride for stride. Sting Ray and Irish brought up the rear. Ben retraced their mad rush through the old part of the city, back to where they'd left the car and driver.

Their escort stood beside the car, an angry frown pushing his jet-black brows together. He had a cell phone pressed to his ear. When he spotted them, he said something and ended the call.

The four of them climbed into the rear of the SUV, their escort sat in the front passenger seat and

133

the driver took them back to the palace.

Leaning close to Ben, she whispered, "I might have a better chance of sneaking that pistol in beneath my *abaya*."

Ben nodded and slipped the gun into her hand.

Yasmin slid it up her sleeve, pulled her arms up inside the garment and settled the weapon into the waistband of the jeans she wore beneath. The challenge would be to hide it somewhere no one in the women's quarters would find it. Though she had a key to her guest apartment, she didn't know who else might have a duplicate. Then she thought of the hidden compartment in her suitcase, where she stored the *thobe* and headdress. The gun would have to fit in there.

The trip back to the palace was uneventful, and soon they were driving through the gates. Yasmin couldn't help thinking it a shame that such a beautiful place could feel so much like a prison. Returning to the palace also meant she'd have to leave Ben.

The driver pulled into the circular front driveway and stopped.

Everyone got out and climbed the steps to the entry.

Yasmin's escort veered toward the women's entrance. When Yasmin didn't follow immediately, he stopped and waited.

"Clearly, he wants me to follow." Yasmin started that direction.

Ben fell in step.

She halted and bent her head, speaking in a low

whisper only he could hear. "I don't need you to escort me. I can make it back to my rooms with the palace escort provided."

"You don't want me to go with you?"

"Of course, I do. But your time would be better spent continuing your search. I'm limited in range during the day."

"Fair enough." He straightened and started to turn away.

"And, Ben?" she said so softly she thought he hadn't heard her.

But, he did. Ben turned back to face her.

"You and the others…" She paused. "Be careful." She wanted to say so much more and to throw her arms around his neck and kiss him, but that couldn't happen. Yasmin walked away, knowing the situation was dire and personal feelings couldn't slow them from accomplishing their mission.

The escort saw her though the door of the east wing. Once inside, Yasmin pulled the veil down from her face and pushed the scarf back behind her.

A couple women lounged in the living area, supervising the play of a three toddlers.

Yasmin smiled in their direction, having completely forgotten their names. She didn't slow until she reached her room, very aware of the gun in her waistband, afraid if she didn't get it out soon, it might fall to the ground in front of one of the women.

Once inside her room, she turned and locked the door. Then she headed straight for the suitcase with the hidden panel. The servants had emptied her cases earlier, but hadn't discovered the hidden compartment. She had the gun safely stowed and the secret panel closed when a knock sounded on her door. Closing the suitcase, she set it on the floor beside the others and hurried to answer.

Erin stood on the other side, a worried frown wrinkling her brow. She darted a glance over her shoulder. "Can we talk?"

"Sure." Yasmin stepped aside and held the door for Erin to enter. Once inside, Yasmin closed the door and locked it again. "What's wrong?" The longer she took to start talking, the more Yasmin's muscles tensed.

Erin paced across the floor, turned and walked back to stand in front of Yasmin. "It's okay, I haven't said anything to Khalid, yet."

"Come, sit." Yasmin led her to a small sofa and urged her to take a seat. Then she sat beside her and took her hands in hers. "I'm sorry if I upset you. I really didn't come here to threaten you or your family."

Erin nodded. "I consider myself a good judge of character, and I don't sense any malice in your words or actions. Frankly, I'm not worried about you. After what you told me, I couldn't sit still, so I went for a walk in the garden to calm my nerves. I happened across Nahla and her sister, Sumbal, talking in a secluded corner. Her sister is married to Khalid's uncle, Bandar. They didn't see me and I...I guess I eavesdropped." She squeezed Yasmin's hands. "They were talking about changes the king has ordered concerning a woman's right to drive."

Yasmin smiled. "Will he allow women to drive?"

Erin nodded. "The decision has the family in an uproar. Sumbal was appealing to Nahla to talk to Khalid, to have him ask the king not to institute this new law. Her husband is against it and thinks it will tear the family apart. He thinks the country is becoming too much like the West. He is in agreement with a movement to remove westerners and democratic ways of thinking from the Arab nation. He wants to reinstitute a more puritanical interpretation of Islamic law with closer connection to Islam."

Yasmin's gut clenched, and she shook her head. "Sounds like a propaganda speech."

Erin snorted. "That's what has me scared. The ideas sounded like what the Islamic State jihadists are preaching."

Exactly what Yasmin thought. "And Prince Bandar Sumbal's husband."

"Yes." Erin touched Yasmin's hand. "I need to talk to my husband. He needs to know what Sumbal and Bandar are saying."

"I wish we could have our hands on the biological weapons before you talk to him." Yasmin sighed. "But, you have to do what you feel is right." She almost asked how she could get a message to Ben, but thought better of it. Her gut told her she could trust Erin, but she didn't want to include the SEAL team on her search for the weapons. As far as anyone knew, the three men she'd come with were paid bodyguards, nothing more. Hopefully, that

137

belief would keep them safe if Yasmin were detained for spying on the royal family.

A knock sounded on the door.

Erin's eyes rounded. "You don't think anyone could have overheard us, do you?" she whispered.

Yasmin shook her head reassuringly and moved toward the exit. "No. Just keep your cool." She twisted the lock and pulled open the door.

Nahla stood on the other side. "Prince Khalid has summoned Erin. Her escort awaits."

Erin leaped to her feet and hurried toward Yasmin. She stopped and hugged her, whispering in her ear, "I'll talk to him. He needs to know."

With a nod, Yasmin released the young woman and stepped back to allow her to pass. "We'll chat later."

Erin covered her red hair and hurried toward the exit.

Nahla stood next to Yasmin for a moment after Erin disappeared, her lips pressed into a tight line. "My son is a good man. He cares about his people, and they care about him."

"He must be a good man. Erin loves him very much," Yasmin observed.

"I did not want to like the Irish wife, but only she loves Khalid as much as I do. Perhaps, more so. She will be a good mother to their children."

"But, her children cannot be considered for the throne?"

"No." Nahla waved her hand. "A successor must be pure Arab."

"Does anyone know why Fatimah cannot get

pregnant?"

"Oh, she can conceive, but she can't carry full term. She has had three miscarriages. The doctor said if she attempts to have any more children, she puts herself at too much risk. Each time, she is gravely ill and nearly dies before her body aborts the baby.

"And I'm here because your son needs an heir." Yasmin's words were more a statement than a question.

Nahla's chin tilted upward. "And to honor a bargain made by his parents and yours. My son is an honorable man."

Eager to get word to Ben, Yasmin eased back into her room. "I just got back from shopping in Riyadh's old market. I'm tired. I'm going to lie down."

Nahla bowed her head. "I am preparing a meal in my quarters. You are welcome to join us."

"Thank you." Yasmin smiled. To be invited to share a meal with the king's wife was a huge step toward acceptance. "I'm honored any other time, but tonight I prefer to skip dinner and sleep."

"If you feel better, please join us." Nahla left to return to her own apartment.

Yasmin entered the guest suite and closed the door. She dug her cell phone out of one of her pockets. Unfortunately, she had no reception. Her radio headset was tucked in her suitcase, next to the gun she'd acquired. She wondered if the radio would pick up through the thick walls. The SEALs had used theirs the night before with some success. And

139

she really needed to get word to Ben.

What Erin had overheard in the garden backed what Omar had told them. Bandar wasn't happy with the way the king was handling things. He'd be even angrier if the king appointed Khalid his successor. That didn't prove Bandar was funding ISIS, or that he was the one who'd purchased biological weapons. But his dissatisfaction with the king's choice of successor was a motive, and a place to start.

Yasmin pulled the tiny radio headset out of the secret compartment of her suitcase, switched it on and stuck it into her ear. She tapped it like she'd seen Ben do. "Hello, can you read me?"

She heard nothing. No voices, nor static. If she wanted to sneak out of the women's quarters without an escort, she'd have to wait until after everyone went to sleep. God, she hoped she didn't have to wait that long. After the altercation in the market, Bandar could be running scared. He could be moving the vials while Yasmin twiddled her thumbs. The situation was unacceptable.

Determined to do something, rather than wait, she pulled the *thobe* and headdress out of her case, took off the *abaya* and dressed in the *thobe*. Then she dragged the black *abaya* over her head, covering all of the white. Where it stuck out beneath the hem, she pulled it up underneath and tucked it into the waistband of her jeans, along with the headdress. If she was careful, she might make it through the shared living area and out of the women's quarters without anyone seeing her. Once outside the

140

women's area, she'd shuck the *abaya*, put on the headdress and find Khalid, hoping her gut wasn't wrong. If Khalid was the one who'd purchased the vials instead of Bandar...well then, she'd have to figure out a way to stay alive long enough to warn someone.

Chapter **Eleven**

BEN, STING RAY AND IRISH met in their room. All they had was their communication devices and the cell phones they'd purchased in Riyadh. They would be playing with fire, searching during the daytime, but Ben had the feeling time was running out. They had to find the vials before the virus left the palace.

Irish fit the radio headset into his ear. "We need to check out the locked doors in the basement. Think it's too risky during the day?"

Sting Ray pounded his fist against his chest. "We're SEALs. We live for danger." Then he ruined the impassioned speech with a grin. "Or so they told us in BUD/S training."

"Whoever brought the vials here had to have stored them somewhere inside the palace," Irish stated.

Ben nodded. "We can start with the basement, since so many people are still moving about. While you two are checking it out, I want a shot at the hidden room. I figure we might be able to search through the palace's regular supper time."

Sting Ray held up a small brick of C-4 plastic explosives. "I think we can get into any locked door with this."

"Damn, Sting Ray." Irish shook his head. "How the hell did you sneak that in?"

Sting Ray shrugged. "I never leave home

without some. You never know when it might be needed."

Ben paced the length of the room and back. "I don't suppose you have a rifle or handgun hidden wherever you had that?"

"Sorry." Sting Ray stuffed the C-4 into one pocket and a few detonators in the other.

"We can use some of that to create a diversion when Big Bird infiltrates the secret room." Irish smiled. "We may not have guns, but maybe these will help." He pulled up his pant leg and unstrapped one of two wicked-looking knives from his calf. "Sting Ray and I picked these up in the market today. Thought they might come in handy."

Ben's chest swelled. The guys were looking out for him. "Thanks. It's getting close to supper time. We should work our way to our positions."

"Will we be missed?"

"If I pass anyone in the hallway, I'll let them know we ate in the market."

Irish rubbed his belly. "Wish I'd known that, and I would have grabbed a bite."

Ben backhanded him in the gut. "You'll live. Let's do this."

They left their quarters and split in the hallway—Ben going one way, Sting Ray and Irish the other.

Ben headed back to the room with the secret door. If he got lucky, he'd get in without being noticed. He passed several palace guards along the way. He nodded toward them and kept going. As he turned a corner, he glanced back.

The guards watched him, but they hadn't followed.

So far, so good.

He made it to the study without incident and knocked on the door. When no one answered, he tried the handle. Locked.

With a file he'd brought from his suitcase, he jimmied the lock, keeping a close eye on the hallway. When an Arab turned the corner and walked his way, Ben dropped to his haunches and pretended to tie his shoe. When he'd finished, he turned away from the door and walked a few steps until the Arab passed out of sight around a corner. Back at the study door, he worked the lock until it clicked open. After a quick glance left and right, he entered. The office was empty. He moved to the side of the door and closed it, and then listened for voices coming from inside the hidden room. Though he didn't hear any, he didn't know how well soundproofed the room might be.

Ben drew in a deep breath and let it out slowly, calming his racing pulse.

Hurrying to the massive mahogany desk, he opened the top drawer and felt inside for the lever or button that would open the door behind the bookcase. The drawer contained several papers, a stapler and some pens. Ben couldn't find the button. He squatted on his haunches and peered into the drawer again.

The button was well hidden, just like the door behind the bookcase. Frustrated and afraid he'd be caught, Ben stood again and felt inside the drawer, this time running his finger along the underside of the desktop. A rounded wooden bump stuck out. He pressed on it and waited. Nothing happened. He waited for the sound of footsteps in the hallway, praying the button wasn't connected to a silent alarm.

No footsteps sounded or voices raised.

He pushed the button harder. This time, it clicked and the wall behind him moved.

Ben stood away from the opening, in case someone was inside and possibly carrying a gun.

The bookcases opened. Lights sprang on, revealing an empty room with a large L-shaped couch, a Persian rug and not much else. Ben entered and checked for doors, drawers, cubbies or a hidden refrigerator where the vials might be stored in. He didn't find anything. The room appeared to be a private meeting chamber. If he had to guess, the walls were insulated to keep sound from coming in or going out.

He wondered if one of the walls led to yet another secret room, but try as he might, he couldn't locate a button, lever or a mechanism to open a wall.

Disappointed, he left the secret room and re-entered the outer office.

Just as the bookshelf doors closed, the doorknob wiggled on the office door.

Ben dove for the back of the tan couch pushed up against the wall and squeezed behind it. If he was lucky, no one would look there. If he wasn't so lucky, someone could discover him and throw him in jail. Pulling his knees to his chest, he scrunched his body into the cramped space and waited, his pulse hammering through his veins, his thoughts churning on a good escape plan should he be discovered.

The hinges made no sound as the door opened, but Ben heard voices speaking Arabic in low tones, talking far too fast for him to translate. He eased to the corner of the sofa and peered around at Prince Khalid and an older man entering through the doorway. His body rubbed against the leather, making a slight squeaking sound.

The older man paused, his gaze swinging toward the sofa.

Ben froze, afraid any movement would cause another squeak.

Prince Khalid spoke and his companion's attention returned to him.

Rashad followed the two men into the room and crossed to the desk, pushed the button and waited for the bookshelves to part.

Khalid waved his hand toward the room. The older man entered. When Rashad started to follow, Prince Khalid faced him and held up his hand.

Rashad frowned but bowed his head and stepped away from the hidden conference room. The bookshelves slid into place.

Ben scooted back out of sight.

The uninvited Rashad paced the length of the office again and again, coming within inches of where Ben hid behind the sofa. At one point, the sound of his footsteps halted on the other side of the room.

Ben dared to peek out from behind the sofa.

The Arab stared at his cell phone, frowning as if reading a text message that wasn't making him happy. He glanced at the bookshelf, and then resumed pacing, faster, with more force in his steps.

New information seemed to have made him angry or anxious. Ben waited for the men to clear the room and allow him to continue his search. Perhaps he'd missed something in the inner sanctum—a sconce, a painting, something that wouldn't be immediately obvious.

Finally, the creak of the wooden bookshelves sliding open came, followed by the voices of the prince and the older man.

Again, Ben peered around the side of the sofa.

Prince Khalid walked beside the older man all the way to the door. The door opened, the prince said one last thing and stepped out, leaving Rashad and the older man in the room to close the door behind him.

Great. Ben lay still, praying the two men would conclude their business and move on.

Instead, they settled into a heated conversation, their words low but insistent. The older man seemed angry. Rashad spoke fast, as if trying to calm him or explain something.

The older Arab made one last, strong, final statement and left the room, slamming the door.

Near the end of his own patience, Ben wondered what was keeping Rashad from leaving. Looking out one last time, he discovered Rashad texting on his cell phone, his thumbs flying over the keys. He hit a button and looked up, shooting a glance around the room before turning toward the sofa behind which Ben lay.

Ben eased back out of sight. His breath caught and held, and he prayed Rashad hadn't seen him.

The door opened and closed.

Waiting a minute longer, listening to the silence, Ben finally poked his head out again. The room was empty. He released the breath he'd held and rose from behind the sofa, vowing to brush up on his Arabic before he deployed to Saudi Arabia again. Whatever Prince Khalid, the older man and Rashad had been discussing seemed to have all three men wound tight.

Ben hoped they hadn't decided on the immediate use of biological warfare.

No matter how many times she glanced out into the living area, Yasmin couldn't catch a break. One or two of the women seemed to always be lounging on a cushion or playing with a child. She wished they would all go to supper soon so she could sneak out. Getting past the guard at the entrance would be the biggest challenge. He was there to keep men from entering the women's quarters, but how would he react if a lone female ventured out without an escort?

The risk was one she'd have to take to get word to Ben about Khalid's uncle. Perhaps they could search his palace apartment. Come to think of it, Yasmin wasn't certain who lived in the prince's palace and who didn't. She didn't know whether Bandar's wife had come to visit Nahla or if she lived somewhere in the palace with Bandar.

Just when she was beginning to think she'd have to walk out like she owned the place, she saw the door open.

One of the male palace staff carried a woman through. The woman's headscarf fell away, revealing red hair and a very pale face.

Yasmin gasped and hurried forward. "Erin?"

The young Irish woman's eyes were closed...no...they were swelled shut, her face battered and bruised, her lips cracked and bleeding.

Yasmin clamped her jaw tight and counted three before asking calmly, "What happened?"

The man shook his head and glanced around. When he spotted the sofa, he carried Erin across the floor and laid her out on the cushions. The servant hurriedly left the room.

Women emerged from their apartments, gathering around Erin.

Yasmin stared down at the sweet, unconscious woman. Her jaw tightened. She'd been summoned to see Prince Khalid. If this was the way a prince treated his wives, the bastard would have no qualms about using biological warfare on unsuspecting populations.

Anger roiled in Yasmin's belly.

Nahla appeared at her side and said a few curt words to Fatimah.

The younger woman pulled her cell phone from her pocket and dialed.

Khalid's mother spoke sharply to another woman, who ran into her apartment and returned with a damp cloth and a bag of ice. Nahla went to work treating Erin's wounds, washing her face and applying ice to her swollen eyes.

Erin remained unconscious, moaning occasionally as her mother-in-law worked.

Torn between staying and helping with Erin and leaving to beat the shit out of whoever did this, Yasmin paced the living area, stopping every pass to check on Erin's progress. *Where's the damned doctor?* She wanted to scream it out loud, but couldn't risk blowing her cover.

The door to the east wing opened, and a woman stepped inside. She wore a white lab coat over loose trousers, a black headscarf and carried a doctor's satchel with a stethoscope around her neck.

Fatimah hurried forward, touched the woman's arm and led her back to where Erin lay on the couch.

She peeled back Erin's eyelids and shone a light on her pupils. Speaking softly in Arabic, the doctor conversed with Nahla, who nodded gravely.

When the doctor rose to leave, Yasmin stepped in front of her. "You can't go. Erin's not awake. What's wrong with her?"

The doctor took a step back and lifted her chin. "The patient has suffered a fall and a possible concussion."

"Fall?" Yasmin snorted. "Maybe she did fall. But only after being beaten. Someone did this to her. Someone hurt her, and you dare to stand there

150

and suggest she had a fall?"

She stared around at all of the women, stopping on Nahla. "Well, the hell with all of you. Erin cares about you and considers you her family. And yet you'd let this abuse go on as if it didn't happen?" She spun on her heels and marched toward the door.

Nahla hurried after her and placed a hand on her arm. "What will you do?"

"Confront the bastard who did this." Yasmin didn't wait for Nahla's response. She wrapped her scarf around her head and neck and charged through the door.

Once on the other side, she sailed past the guard, too angry to worry about what he might do. If he tried to stop her, then she'd take him down and move on.

The guard didn't attack. Yasmin pulled her scarf up around her ear, forming a veil over her mouth and nose. As soon as she could, she ducked into an empty sitting room, stripped off the *abaya*, tucked her hair beneath the red-checkered headdress and planted the black braid on top to hold the cloth in place. When she felt certain she looked sufficiently like one of the men, she hid the *abaya* in a potted plant and checked the hallway for traffic.

An older man with a salt-and-pepper beard hurried down the hallway, his heavy brows pulled into a deep frown.

After he passed, Yasmin continued toward Prince Khalid's quarters, anger driving her through the many corridors until she found one more

151

opulent than the rest. The one belonging to the prince. The bastard.

How could he profess to love a woman and then beat her to within an inch of her life?

Yasmin meant to tell him exactly what she thought about men who abused women. She might beat *him* to within an inch of his sorry life. Then, maybe he'd confess to where he'd hidden the vials of virus.

She'd been wrong about the prince, thinking he couldn't possibly have purchased the vials. Erin had convinced her that Khalid was forward thinking, kind, and caring about his people and helping them fit into a changing world.

Ha!

In front of her, the prince emerged from a room and turned away from her, his footsteps carrying him quickly in the opposite direction.

Yasmin ducked her head and sped up, following the prince to the end of a long hallway. When she saw him enter another doorway, she sprinted the last couple of steps and slammed into the door behind him before it closed.

As soon as she was through the door, she was grabbed and yanked backward. A dark, muscular arm clamped around her neck and shut off the air to her lungs.

Yasmin fought, kicked, and struggled, but she couldn't dislodge the arm, nor flip the guy over her shoulder.

Prince Khalid appeared in front of her and spoke sharply in Arabic.

When she didn't respond, the prince stared closer, his brows descending. He raised a hand.

Yasmin flinched and closed her eyes.

Instead of hitting her, he ripped off the headdress and threw it to the floor. "Aliya, what is the meaning of this intrusion? And why are you wearing a man's clothing?"

Yasmin pulled at the arm around her neck, her vision blurring.

The prince rapped out an order in Arabic.

The man holding her released her so fast, she nearly fell to the floor. As soon as the fog around her vision cleared, she launched herself at Prince Khalid, shoving him hard in the chest.

He glared at her. "What are you doing?"

"Showing you what it's like to be pushed around." She pushed him again.

That muscular arm clamped around her neck again and pulled her off the prince.

Holding a hand to his chest, Prince Khalid frowned. "Are you insane? Why have you attacked me?"

"That's not all I'm going to do. After what you did to Erin, you deserve to be pounded into a bloody pulp, you sorry bastard!"

The angry frown drawing his dark brows together deepened, and he grabbed her arm. "What about Erin? What happened?"

"You damn well know. You're the one who beat her unconscious. That poor woman loves you enough to give up the life she knows, to share you with other women in a country that treats its women like cattle. This is how you repay her?" Yasmin fought against the arm holding her back.

Khalid backed a step, his eyes widening. "I have to see Erin."

His shocked reaction didn't hold true for a man who'd beat his wife, but Yasmin was too mad to stop. "Why? So you can hit her again? Leave her alone!" Yasmin kicked out, hoping to land another blow.

Khalid nodded to the man holding her.

The man released her.

Khalid grabbed her arms and held her firmly away. "I didn't beat Erin. I would never harm the woman I love with all of my heart."

Anger still roiling inside, Yasmin stared into the prince's eyes, unsure about trusting him, not after the way Erin had returned to her quarters.

His grip tightened. "I wouldn't hurt my wife."

Noting the sincerity of the lines of concern around his eyes, Yasmin had to believe the prince. The shock and anger radiating from him could not have been faked.

His jaw hardened and a fierce look glowed in his narrowed eyes. "I will find out who hurt her and take care of this incident." Prince Khalid stormed toward the door, breaking into a jog before he cleared the doorway. He shouted something over his shoulder in Arabic.

The prince's bodyguard sprinted after him, leaving Yasmin alone. She pressed a hand to her throat, glad she'd lived through the bodyguard's display of loyalty to the Saudi prince. Yasmin hoped

154

Prince Khalid found the bastard who'd beaten Erin. If he truly loved her, he'd find the bastard and make him pay.

In the meantime, Yasmin had to find Ben and let him know what Nahla's sister had said about her husband's desire to halt the westernization of their country. The man had to be angry that the king had deliberately passed over him to designate Khalid as the next ruler of Saudi Arabia. If anyone had a motive to cause trouble, that person was Prince Bandar.

Yasmin pulled back her hair, settled the red-checkered headdress on her had with the black braid and peeked out the door into an empty hallway. With no one to stop her, she turned in the opposite direction as Prince Khalid and his guard and continued down the hall. Rounding a corner, she spotted Rashad entering a room.

Yasmin slowed and waited until Rashad disappeared inside before she hurried down the corridor. She'd almost made it past the entrance to the room when an arm snagged hers and yanked her through the opening.

Yasmin bunched her muscles, ready to fight. Instead of calling for help, she planted her feet on the smooth tile floor, grabbed the hand holding her arm and bent double—all in a practiced move she'd learned during self-defense training.

The man holding her flipped over her shoulder and landed on his back with a thud.

Not wanting to call attention to her plight and have the entire palace aware she'd disguised herself

155

as a man, Yasmin made a run for the exit.

Before she reached it, a figure in black sprang out of nowhere and slammed into her side, sending her flying into the doorframe. Yasmin threw her arms up in front of her, but too late. Her head hit solid wood, pain shot through her temple and darkness claimed her

Chapter **Twelve**

SURE HE'D MISSED something in the hidden room, Ben waited until Rashad left the study and then raced across the floor, opened the desk drawer and hit the button.

The bookshelves slid open, and Ben entered. Somewhere, there had to be a secret compartment, perhaps another hidden doorway or switch that opened a panel in the wall.

Ben focused his attention on the large, L-shaped couch in the middle of the room. Nowhere on the couch was a switch, lever or button. He lifted the Persian rug, searching for a trap door. Nothing.

Again, he ran his hand along the wall and pulled at the ornate sconces, almost ripping them down.

"Big Bird," Irish's voice said into the headset in Ben's ear.

"Go ahead." Ben listened while he continued to run his hands across the wall. He came to a mural of a silver Arabian horse rearing on its hindquarters. As he ran his fingers across the horse's painted hoof, he felt an indentation. The light and shadows of the painting hid the hollow well.

"We found a kind of warehouse in one of the locked rooms in the basement."

"Anything interesting in it?"

"We're on to something down here."

Ben could hear the excitement in Irish's voice, and his pulse ratcheted up a notch. At the same time, he pushed on the depression in the wall. He could hear the hum of a motor and the metallic sound of gears turning. Ben glanced behind him. The entire floor beneath the couch and Persian rug rose into the air, revealing a spiral staircase winding downward to a darkened space below the hidden room. "Have you located the vials?" Ben asked, crossing to the staircase.

"Not yet, but I'd bet my boots we'll find them in here."

"Let me know. I've discovered another hidden access leading downward. Maybe into the basement. I'll let you know what's down there." Ben pulled a small flashlight from his jeans pocket, switched the lens to red to make it harder for someone to see him coming, and started down the stairs. If there was a room below, it was cloaked in darkness, which was fine with Ben. Lack of light meant no one was in the room at that time.

The staircase wound around and around until it emptied onto a bare concrete floor. Ben shone his light around the room, which was nothing more than concrete walls and a door leading somewhere else. His guess was that this might be an escape route to get people out of the palace or to a safe room below.

Once his weight was off the last step, the staircase and the floor above lowered, closing him into the concrete bunker. Ben located a switch on the wall. He flipped it upward and the staircase and ceiling rose. His heartbeat sped. What if he couldn't get the staircase to come back down?

He flipped the switch down and it descended. *Whew!* At least, he knew he could go back the way he'd come, if needed.

"There is a series of rooms off the warehouse," Irish reported. "I had to use the C-4 to blast through the lock on the first one. It's the armory, with a cache of rifles, grenade launchers and machine guns."

"Nice to know." Ben entered a tunnel-like hallway, walked to the end and faced a solid metal door. He turned the handle and eased it open. As he did, lights sprang on, illuminating another hallway painted bright white with doors leading off each side. He opened the first one to find a small room with concrete walls. It smelled like old sweat socks and urine, with a hint of a metallic bite. Ben's gut knotted. This room was, or had been, a cell.

The next room was the same, and the next. On the other side of the hallway, he found more cells. The good news was they were all empty.

Another heavy metal door ended the hallway. He twisted the knob, but it was locked. With the metal file he'd brought from his kit, he worked the lock until he heard the solid click and the door swung open into a larger room.

Anger simmered inside Ben. Shackles hung from the walls and were anchored in the concrete floor. Chains dangled from the ceiling.

Ben's fists clenched as he passed through what he could only imagine was a torture chamber. The floors were clean of blood and excrement, but the smell lingered. He hurried through to the next door.

By then, Ben had the knack for picking locks and made quick work of tripping the latch in the doorknob. On the opposite side of the door, he noted heavy deadbolt locks.

The door opened into a huge room, with pallets of boxes and a forklift. Soft footsteps sounded on the concrete floor.

Ben ducked behind a stack of cardboard boxes and waited for the person to pass. He held his breath and listened carefully.

The sound of footfalls stopped. After a few moments, they started again, heading his direction.

Bunching his muscles, he prepared to spring at his opponent.

A figure rounded the stack of boxes and shoved the barrel of an AK47 into his face.

Ben's heart leaped into his throat, and he froze.

"Damn it," Irish said. "I could have killed you."

Ben's gaze traveled the length of the barrel, and he let go of the breath he'd been holding. "You almost didn't need to. I almost had a heart attack when you stuck that thing in my face." He straightened and looked past Irish. "Where's Sting Ray?"

"Guys, I found them," Sting Ray's voice said into Ben's radio headset.

"Where?" Ben stepped around the pallet of boxes.

"Back of the warehouse, last door on the left. A lab of sorts."

"On our way." Ben followed Irish through the maze of boxes, furniture, and supplies needed to run the prince's palace. As they approached the open door, Ben heard voices echoing off the ceiling. He turned and peered down a long gap between stacks of boxes to see five men enter the warehouse, talking and laughing.

One climbed onto a forklift and revved the propane-powered engine. The others went to work moving boxes.

Ben stepped into the room, grabbed Irish's arm and dragged him inside, closing the door behind them. "We've got company."

"Yeah, and we have the vials." Sting Ray held up a canister marked with the name of the pharmaceutical company and the green dove emblem on the side.

"How do you know it's the virus?" Ben asked.

His hands encased in HAZMAT gloves, Sting Ray turned the canister so Ben could see the skull and crossbones gracing the other side. "They were locked cabinet in that room over there." He pointed to a door on the other side of a glass window.

"Are you sure it's safe to handle?" Irish asked.

"Hell, no." Sting Ray held the cylinder away from his body. "I'm guessing the canister is keeping it contained, for the time being."

Ben found a large insulated bag in a cabinet and held it open. "Put it in here." Once Sting Ray deposited the canister into the bag, the three men scoured the room for anything else that might appear dangerous.

"We need to get out of here with this," Sting Ray said. "The sooner, the better. You think the

161

prince will miss his fiancée if we up and leave the palace without a word?"

"We'll have to time it better than that. Getting away from the palace might not be as hard as getting out of the country."

"First things first," Ben said. "We have to get back to our rooms without being discovered."

Irish shook his head. "The guys in the warehouse are blocking our exit. They could be there for a while."

Ben nodded. "I have another way out. Follow me." He slung the strap of the insulated bag over his shoulder and opened the door a crack.

The sound of the forklift hummed at the other end of the warehouse.

Ben poked his head out farther. When he didn't see the other men moving around, he ran for the cover of a stack of boxes. From there, he checked the length of an aisle between the stacks of goods. When he determined it, too, was clear, he ran for the far wall, ducking and dodging between boxes and furniture until he arrived at the door he'd come through a few minutes before.

Sting Ray and Irish shadowed his trail.

As Ben ducked through the door, he heard a shout echo in the warehouse.

Footsteps pounded on concrete, heading their direction.

Damn. They'd been discovered. The only way they might get out of this without being caught was if they made it through to the hidden room first.

Once Irish and Sting Ray were through the

door, Ben jammed a blade of his pocketknife into the lock and broke it off. The disabled door would hold them off for a short time, but his team still had to get all of the way back without being found in an obviously forbidden place, in possession of the deadly pet project of one of the members of the royal family.

Ben ran through the torture chamber, toward the door leading into the cells. He reached for the handle and turned it. Just as he was about to fling open the door, he heard an angry male voice on the other side.

Trapped between the warehouse men and the guy in the hallway to the cells, Ben turned to Sting Ray and Irish. "Looks like we might have to fight our way out of this one."

Yasmin came to as she was dropped onto a cold, hard concrete floor. She blinked open her eyes and stared up the man who'd carried her into what appeared to be a stark cell without windows. The same man who'd been her escort on the plane ride over from London. Rashad.

He spoke heatedly to someone standing behind him, someone she couldn't see. Gathering as much self-righteous anger as she could with her throbbing head, Yasmin demanded, "Rashad, what is the meaning of this?"

He glared down at her, a snarl curling his lips. "You are not fit to be a princess. Most certainly, you are not fit to marry Prince Khalid."

"You have your opinion." She bowed her head

163

demurely. "I would think the prince will make that choice, not you."

"He is not fit to be king of our great country. He is young and foolish."

"And who should be king, Rashad?" Yasmin tried to keep the man talking so she could think through the cloud of pain for a way to escape.

Another face appeared in the doorway. Sumbal. "The man who should be king. A man who knows what this country needs. My husband."

Yasmin nodded at the woman, remembering what Erin told her. "You are the wife of Prince Bandar."

She lifted her chin. "I am. He will banish the westerners from poisoning the minds of our young. He will bring a return of Islam to our people, and remove the infidels from among us."

"You were the one who hit me and knocked me unconscious?" Yasmin rubbed her forehead and winced.

Sumbal nodded. "I am. You are a disgrace to the House of Saud. My nephew would be making a mistake in marrying you." She snorted. "A spy among us. Women were not meant to dress as men and sneak into places where they are not invited."

Yasmin bowed her head, allowing the woman berate her, giving her even more time to think through her plan of action. With no weapons within reach, Yasmin had no other choice but to attack with all her might. Bunching her muscles, Yasmin pushed to a standing position and waited for her head to quit spinning. "Do you really want a return of Islam, or is it that you just want your husband to be king?"

Sumbal's dark eyes narrowed and her nostrils flared. "You will never know." She darted a glance toward Rashad. "Are you going to kill her?"

Rashad nodded.

"Good." Sumbal spun and started for the door.

Yasmin launched herself at the woman like a football player going in for the tackle. She hit Sumbal in the middle of her back, sending her flying into Rashad's chest. He staggered backward and fell, with Sumbal landing on top of him.

Yasmin leaped over them, but she didn't make it to the door before Rashad caught her ankle.

Momentum carried her body over the pair, but the hand on her ankle brought her up short, and she landed on her chest, the air knocked from her lungs. Yasmin yanked her ankle free and crawled a few steps away, coming up on her hands and knees. Before she could rise to her feet, Rashad landed on her back, pinning her to the floor with the weight of his body.

She bucked and fought, but he had her.

"Kill her," Sumbal yelled. "Or I will!"

Rashad pulled a knife from his belt and pressed it to Yasmin's throat, the tip slicing into her skin. This was the end. She'd die at the hand of her enemy without seeing Ben again. Without the opportunity to tell him she thought he was handsome and trustworthy. And so good in bed.

Rashad jerked backward with a grunt and sprawled across the floor on his back.

Yasmin rolled to her side and stared up through the haze of pain throbbing in her temples at what appeared to be an enraged Norse god. "Ben?" she said, blinking. "Where did you come from?" Then she passed out

Chapter Thirteen

BEN SWUNG TOWARD the door leading into the cell block. Hopefully the cell block would contain fewer people. They could subdue them, sneak back through to the staircase and up into the hidden room. With only a short window of time to work with, they had to get out, grab Yasmin and leave the palace before the alarm went up announcing intruders had escaped from the warehouse into the main palace.

They wouldn't get far once the alarm spread through the palace.

He pulled the door open and braced himself for a fight.

The corridor stood empty, but he could hear voices coming from one of the cells near the staircase.

He pressed a finger to his lips and motioned for the others to maintain their silence. Then he eased forward, passing one cell after the other until he arrived at the one that had voices coming from within.

A woman said something in Arabic. Even Ben's rusty skills could translate the words.

Are you going to kill her?

Without a doubt, Ben knew who the "her" was. Taking a deep breath, he eased his head around the edge of the door and peered into the shadowy interior of one of the cells. Rashad kneeled over the crumpled body of a woman. He held a knife in his hand and pressed the tip against the woman's throat.

Blood chilled in Ben's veins. The person lying on the ground wore a thobe and had long, black hair and olive-toned skin.

His gut clenching, Ben pushed aside diplomacy and negotiation skills and went for brute force. He rushed into the room, grabbed Rashad by the back of his collar and yanked him off Yasmin, flinging him against the wall.

In the next moment, a screaming banshee, dressed in a black *abaya,* launched herself into him, knocking him off his feet.

He crashed to the ground with a grunt and rolled to the side as the female landed beside him.

She pushed to her feet and rushed him again.

Not wanting to kill her, but not wanting to lose his life trying to save the life of an insane woman, he caught her, lifted her off the ground and flung her to the far wall. She hit the hard, stone wall and slid to the ground.

Ben glanced around for additional threats.

"We're clear. Check our girl." Irish stood on one side of Rashad, holding the man's arm up behind his back in what Ben knew to be a painful position. Sting Ray stood guard over the woman in the black *abaya*, holding the containers of virus in his gloved hands.

Ben dropped to his haunches beside Yasmin and felt for a pulse. His pulse thundered through his system, pounding loudly against his eardrums. For a long moment, he didn't feel the reassuring thumping of blood pumping through her veins. Then it was there. Th-thump. Th-thump.

He let go of the breath he'd been holding and brushed the hair from Yasmin's face. "Hey, pretty lady, wake up." He touched her shoulder gently, but she didn't open her eyes. His gut knotted all over again. She could have a concussion or swelling on the brain. "We need to get her to a doctor. ASAP." Ben gathered her into his arms and lifted her. He'd carry her all the way to the States if he had to, but he wasn't going to let her die. Not here. Not now. In the few short days he'd known this woman, she'd touched him in a way he hadn't known was possible. She couldn't die now. He wanted her to continue touching him in that exact same way and more. And he wanted to touch her sweet body all over again. Preferably when she was conscious and moaning his name in passion, not pain.

"What now?" Sting Ray asked.

"How are we going to explain what happened here to the rest of the palace?" Irish swung Rashad out of the way of the exit.

Ben stepped out in the corridor and hit the lever that lowered the stairs to the hidden room. "I don't care how we do it, but we're getting Yasmin help. Now."

When Yasmin came to again, she lay on a bed with a cool compress draped across her forehead. As the events of the day came back to her, she sat up straight, clapped a hand to her cheek and stared around the room. Her gaze landed on Nahla, kneeling on a cushion on the floor nearby.

When she saw Yasmin's eyes were open, the older woman rose to her feet. "Ah, you are coming out of it."

"Out of what?" Yasmin shifted and a stabbing pain ripped through her head. She shut her eyes and moaned.

"You have been asleep for over a day. Everyone has been worried about you."

"A day?" Yasmin sat up, but her head spun and she lay back down. "Where's Ben? Is he all right?"

"Your bodyguards are quite well and being treated like kings by Prince Khalid." Nahla smiled. "They stopped a very bad thing from happening, and for that, I am grateful."

Yasmin's eyes widened and she dared to let her heart soar. Could it be true? Had the guys succeeded in finding the vials? "What very bad thing?"

"When they learned you were missing, they went in search of you. Not only did they help save you from certain death, they found a canister of deadly virus, one of our own had purchased as a weapon of mass destruction."

A huge weight lifted as relief washed over Yasmin. She sank back against the mattress, a smile spreading across her face. They'd found the virus.

Nahla nodded once. "It is being destroyed, as we speak, in a special incinerator."

Yasmin closed her eyes and sent a silent prayer of thanks to the heavens. "I'm glad. No one should have access to that kind of weapon. It is far too dangerous."

"Agreed. And my son agrees. He is thankful your bodyguards saved you before Rashad and Sumbal could kill you." Nahla smoothed a hand over Yasmin's hair. "We heard of your attempt to escape. You are truly a fierce warrior princess, destined to be a great queen."

Yasmin hated lying to this woman who'd been so kind and welcoming. "About that…"

"You should rest. Your bodyguards have been asking about you. I will inform them of your awakening."

Her head still throbbing from banging it twice, Yasmin didn't feel like arguing. She closed her eyes and slept.

Sunlight streamed across her face, warm and insistent. Yasmin blinked open her eyes and stared up at the ceiling, disoriented for a moment, wondering where she was. The events of the past few days flooded over her, and she sighed.

"That was a big sigh," a female voice said.

Yasmin turned her head, the stabbing pain from the last time she'd woken having receded into a dull throb.

Erin sat on a cushion beside the bed, squinting through her swollen eyes. The bruises on her face were still bright blue and purple with a hint of yellow on the edges, already healing.

"Hey," Yasmin said, surprised at how hoarse she sounded.

"I gave Nahla a break. She's been with since they brought you back to your room."

"You don't have to sit with me. I'm fine. *You're*

the one we should be waiting on." Yasmin pushed to a sitting position, happy she didn't feel like passing out or throwing up. "How are you?"

Erin grinned and winced, pressing a hand to her busted lip. "Fine, as long as I don't smile. Actually, I'm better than fine. Khalid has been by my side for much of the past twenty-four hours. He was so upset by what happened, he held me for hours and wouldn't let anyone else get close."

Yasmin hugged Erin. "I'm happy for you."

Erin ducked her head. "Khalid told his father he didn't want to be king. He wants to be free to live his life as he sees fit. He's granting Fatimah a divorce."

Her heart contracting, Yasmin touched Erin's arm. "How does Fatimah feel about it?"

"I never knew how unhappy she was. She's going to university in England." Erin leaned close. "And, if you ask me, I don't think she will come back. I think she's been reading forbidden romance novels and wants to fall in love with a handsome man." She smiled again, winced and pressed a finger to her split lip.

"I'm happy for her," Yasmin said. "But what about you? Did they find out who beat you?"

Erin's brows drew together. "Sumbal put Rashad up to it. He wore a hood. I couldn't see who it was beneath." Her breath caught on a sob and she looked away, tears leaking from her eyes. "He said I was the reason Khalid and the king were ruining the country. I needed to leave Khalid. He would be better off without me. I was almost convinced, until

Khalid came to my side."

"Was Prince Bandar behind Sumbal's attempt to kill me?"

"Prince Bandar swears he knew nothing about what Rashad and Sumbal were up to. He disavows any knowledge of how the virus came to be in the palace. Sumbal hasn't spoken since she was taken away, and Rashad is in jail. He confessed to the purchase of the virus. He wanted to use it against non-Muslims." Erin shook her head. "A virus doesn't care what religion you are. It will attack anyone."

The redhead pushed to her feet. "Enough about conspiracies and viruses. I have a surprise for you." Erin left the room and returned a few minutes later. She held open the door and grinned. "I sneaked him in. He was determined to prove to himself you were really alive and well."

Ben entered, a sexy smile curling his lips.

Yasmin smiled at the man who filled the room with his incredible height and breadth of shoulders.

"Oh, and thank you for going to Khalid about what happened to me." Erin's cheeks blossomed with pink. "He's never been more loving and attentive. He wasn't even disappointed to learn you weren't Aliya."

"And I was the one who told him you weren't marrying him," Ben said. "Erin's right. The man seemed relieved. Had he heard what a hardass you are?"

Eyebrows raised, Erin glanced from Ben to Yasmin. "Do you want me to stay?"

"No!" Ben and Yasmin said as one.

Erin laughed. "Okay, okay. I get it. I'm leaving." She walked out of the room and pulled the door closed.

Ben dropped to his knees beside the bed and took her hand in his. "So, the wedding is off. You'll have to go to Plan B."

"Plan B?"

"Back to square one, start dating other men." Ben jabbed his thumb toward his chest. "Or, rather, another man. Me."

"And why would I want to date a SEAL? You guys are never home, you're always hanging out together and you break women's hearts all over the world."

Ben nodded. "Yeah, we do, don't we?" He gave her a sweet smile. "I requested leave for when we fly back to London." He lifted her hand and pressed it to his cheek, the stubble rough against her skin.

"You did?" she asked absently, her thoughts spinning around her hand where he massaged her fingers, heat pooling low in her belly. "What if I don't want to go out with you?" Which was a big fat lie.

"Oh, you do," he said. "Yeah, it's crazy to think we can make a relationship work. Especially with our insane schedules and assignments, but I'm willing to do this if you are."

Yasmin bit her lip and studied him. Her mouth worked without engaging her brain. "I'm in." Gut instinct had made the decision, and her heart couldn't be happier. She smiled and pressed a kiss to his knuckles. "I might even swing a transfer from my London office back to the States. That's how in I am. Now, kiss me before I change my mind." Not that she would. This was a man who could put up with her lifestyle. A man who wouldn't ask her to change. A man who was honest, loyal and so very caring.

Yeah, she was in it for the long haul, and she couldn't wait to get to some place where she could make love to this man all night long.

"I'm ready to go back to London, now," she said, pulling down his head so she could kiss him.

He claimed her lips, tracing the seam with the tip of his tongue. She opened to him, and he slid into her mouth and caressed her in a long, slow, wet glide.

Sweet heaven, she wanted him inside her. Now. "Do we have to wait until we get back to London?" she whispered.

"Hell no, we don't." Ben slipped onto the bed beside her and skimmed a hand down the front of her nightgown. "We might go to jail for this. Are you concerned?"

She grabbed his hand and guided it to the juncture of her thighs. "Only one concern."

"Just one?"

"Yeah. You're wearing too many clothes. How long does it take to get a SEAL naked?"

Epilogue

BEN ROLLED OVER in the king-sized bed he'd had moved into his apartment in Little Creek, Virginia, his eyes closed, his hands reaching for Yasmin. When he didn't find smooth, soft skin, he moved farther over. "Damned bed is too big," he groused and opened his eyes. "Can't find my woman."

"Because I'm not in the bed, you big goof." A naked Yasmin entered the bedroom, carrying a tray with coffee mugs and what smelled like eggs and toast. "I was hungry, so I made breakfast.

His already hardening cock sprang to complete attention, jutting toward the ceiling. Ben leaned up against the headboard and crossed his arms behind his head. "About time I got you trained."

Yasmin's brows rose up her forehead. "Watch it, frogman. You don't want hot coffee spilled on your privates. And don't get used to this. I prefer when you bring *me* breakfast in bed. It's much more interesting."

Ben grinned and held out his hands for the tray. He set the tray on the nightstand, freeing his hands and hers for better things to come. "So you liked whipped cream with your waffles?"

Yasmin's smile spread across her face as she climbed into the bed beside him. "On my waffles and practically everywhere else you could find a place to put it. She reached for the can of whipped

176

cream on the tray. "I thought it would go good with the coffee."

His hand beat hers to the can and he held it out of her reach. "Me first."

She pouted, something new she'd picked up since she'd moved into his apartment. She said she'd learned it from one of the porn movies she found in his bottom drawer—a leftover from his bachelor days. "I had the perfect spot for a dollop of cream." She tilted her head, eyeing his distended cock. "I promise to lick it all off." Yasmin curled her fingers around his shaft and ran her hand down its length. "What did you have in mind?"

Ben thought he'd come right then, but he held tight, knowing this was only the beginning. If he wanted to make her as hot as he was, he had to make it last. "I had this in mind." He leaned over and squirted a creamy puff onto her nipple. The he sucked it and her nipple into his mouth and flicked her breast clean. God, she tasted better than the whipped cream.

Ben raised his head to capture her lips, sliding his tongue the length of hers until he had to break it off to breathe. "No regrets about leaving your posh London office?" he said against her mouth.

Yasmin snorted softly. "Hardly. Now I can have my waffles with whipped cream, and then have you for desert." She pushed him onto his back, slung her leg over his hips and straddled him. "Frogman, if you don't mind, I'd rather skip breakfast and get straight to the desert."

Ben grinned and reached into the nightstand

for one of the many condoms he kept handy for just such an occasion. "By all means, I can't keep the lady waiting."

"Damn right. I actually have to go to work today. And so do you. Vacation is over." She ripped the package open and rolled the protection over his rock-hard dick and then rose up on her knees, positioning herself over him. "But not before we rock the bedsprings. A girl can't get too much exercise. They say you can burn more calories having sex than walking a mile."

"I'm willing to test the theory."

"Good. Because otherwise, I'd have to sweeten you up with whipped cream until you came...around to my way of thinking."

"Enough talk. How about a little more action?" He gripped her hips in his hands and brought her down over him, sliding his cloaked staff into her slick channel.

Yasmin tipped her head backward and moaned. "Oh yes. Saving your ass in that bar in London turned out to be..." she sucked in a strangled breath as he moved inside her, "a damned good decision." She lowered herself all the way down, taking him fully into her.

Ben moaned. "You saved my ass? I think it was the other way around."

"You want to do it the other way around?" She rose up his shaft.

His fingers tightened on her hips. "No. I want you right where you are."

"I could stay like this forever." She leaned her

hands on his chest. "Think you could handle that?"

Ben's heart swelled and his dick got even harder. "Baby, I know I could. You're the best thing that ever happened to me, and I want to keep you for as long as you'll let me. But—" He pulled her down until he could slide his lips across hers. "With your appetite, we'd better stock up on condoms."

About the Author

ELLE JAMES also writing as MYLA JACKSON is a *New York Times* and *USA Today* Bestselling author of books including cowboys, intrigues and paranormal adventures that keep her readers on the edges of their seats. With over eighty works in a variety of sub-genres and lengths she has published with Harlequin, Samhain, Ellora's Cave, Kensington, Cleis Press, and Avon. When she's not at her computer, she's traveling, snow skiing, boating, or riding her ATV, dreaming up new stories.

To learn more about Elle James and her stories visit her website at http://www.ellejames.com.

To learn more about Myla Jackson visit her websites at www.mylajackson.com

DELIVERANCE

New York Times & USA Today Bestselling Author

ELLE JAMES

SEAL'S DELIVERANCE

TAKE NO PRISONERS

BOOK #9

ELLE JAMES

New York Times & USA Today
Bestselling Author

About This Book

Navy SEAL and a sexy CDC biologist join forces in Montana to find the one responsible for threatening revenge on the SEAL team's loved ones through biological terrorism

Raymond "Sting Ray" Thompson returns home to Eagle Rock, Montana, when a trail of treachery leads him back with members of his SEAL team. Their mission: to locate the biological terrorist targeting people closest to them. Claiming retribution for destroying an Ethiopian factory generating a deadly virus, the terrorist strikes Sting Ray's uncle, the man who raised him. His team joins forces with a group of former military men to ferret out the terrorist and halt the release of the deadly virus into the environment.

On vacation from her job with the CDC, Lilly Parker is with her brother in Montana when she gets the call to investigate a potential biological disaster targeting a family member of a Navy SEAL. Working with the Brotherhood Protectors and a team of Navy SEALs, Lilly conducts a covert investigation. Lilly and Sting Ray join forces to trace the virus to its source, determined to contain the disaster and protect the community, while fighting their mutual attraction.

Chapter One

Ray Thompson—Sting Ray to his teammates—
slowed as he neared the apartment complex in Little
Creek, Virginia where he kept the few belongings
he'd acquired since he'd joined SEAL Team 10 four
years previously. He glanced at the complex, each
entrance exactly the same as the others, every
apartment the same size and shape, only
differentiated by what the occupants brought to
furnish the interiors.

None of his belongings were worth much. He'd
picked them up in thrift stores or the nearby
warehouse-style superstore. None of it mattered.
Nothing made it feel like a home. The apartment
served only one purpose—it was a place to park his
gear between assignments.

If he had to transfer to another base, he would
call the local women's shelter and have them pick up
the microfiber futon, mattress, boxed springs and
flat screen television he watched the Denver
Broncos on when he was in town during football
season. Yeah, it wasn't much, but he liked it that
way. He'd never really felt like his uncle's place was
home—no warmth, no deep affection, no reason to
return—and it made it easier when he got orders to
ship out.

Home. Since getting back from his fifth
deployment in as many months, this last one to the

1

sands of Riyadh, Saudi Arabia, he'd been thinking more about home. His teammates were all falling in love and settling into their lives with their women. The Friday nights of bar-hopping and Sunday beer, pizza and football were less and less frequent and now included females in the once all-male group dynamic.

Sting Ray couldn't begrudge his battle buddies their newfound happiness. Some men found the women of their dreams. And his teammates had found some beautiful women who were as strong and just as dedicated to making the world a better place as SEAL Team 10. But he thought he'd fallen down that rabbit hole called love once, got burned and had the scars to prove it.

No thanks. He liked being single. He didn't have to check with his woman to know whether he could go out for a beer or watch the game on his own television. Now, sex was another thing entirely. Although he'd given up on relationships, he hadn't given up on nature's best form of stress relief. He just hadn't met anyone lately who tempted him.

Looking back, he wasn't sure he'd been committed to any relationship. If he was fair to his ex-girlfriend, he had to admit to being distant and non-communicative. He blamed that on his uncle. The man had rarely talked.

Before girlfriends, one or two of his teammates who lived in the same apartment complex would run with him. Lately, they preferred to exercise in bed into the late mornings on weekends. Especially since they'd returned from their latest assignment at a Saudi Arabian prince's palace in Riyadh. They'd helped the prince dodge a major biological warfare bullet aimed at the royal family.

The four-man team had secretly made it in, and come out relatively unscathed, having located the vial of toxic virus before it could be unleashed on anyone.

A lot of African villagers hadn't been so lucky. The biological weapon of mass destruction had been tested on entire isolated villages in Somalia and Ethiopia. Not a solitary soul lived to tell who had done it or how. Fortunately, their search had uncovered the manufacturing source and shut it down. But not before several vials had made their way out of the facility.

Sting Ray stretched and stared around the neighborhood of tightly-packed houses and apartment complexes. He'd personally witnessed the horrible devastation to one small, African village. He couldn't imagine the destruction that would occur, if one of those vials were unleashed in Little Creek, Virginia.

Back on American soil, he could almost forget such dangers existed. But there was always another bad guy to stop. And he'd be ready for it, mentally and physically. He wondered what their next assignment might be. Having run five miles that morning, he still had to shower and change into his uniform before he reported to the Naval Base and his team that morning.

Tires screeched behind him.

About to step off the sidewalk and into the

3

parking lot of the apartment building, Sting Ray stepped back in time to keep from walking into a black, crew-cab, four-by-four pickup barreling to a stop in front of him.

He jumped back and yelled, "God damn you, Irish! You almost ran over me."

Irish, one of his teammates, stuck his head out of the window, his face grim. "Get in," he said, jerking his head toward the back door. "We have serious trouble."

The grim expression on his teammate's face washed Sting Ray's anger away in an instant. He flung open the back door, slid in and nodded to Ben "Big Bird" Sjodin, who filled the front seat, wearing an old North Dakota Fighting Sioux T-shirt and jogging shorts.

"What's up?" Sting Ray asked, his deployment meter on high-alert. "Are we shipping out?"

Irish nodded. "Looks like it." He glanced in the rearview mirror. "Have you checked your phone or text messages in the last fifteen minutes?"

Sting Ray frowned and glanced at the cell phone strapped to his arm. Yeah, he'd felt it vibrate a minute or two ago, but he'd been so close to his apartment complex he hadn't bothered to stop and check the message, figuring his boss or teammates would text twice in a row if it had been an actual emergency. Or better still, they would have set off his phone finder alarm and blasted his eardrums. "I haven't. Why? Did I miss anything?"

Big Bird turned in his seat to look back at Sting Ray. "You might have. I'd check it if I were you."

Sting Ray pulled the phone from the strap on his arm, entered his screen lock password and brought up his text messages. At the top of the messages was a text from an unknown number. He opened the text and read, a chill creeping across his sweat-soaked skin.

You took something of value from me
Now, I will take something of value from you
Someone you care about

Sting Ray glanced up, his gaze connecting with Big Bird's. "You know about this?"

Big Bird nodded. "I got one just like it. I called Yasmin immediately. She's on her way to meet us at Irish's apartment. Claire's there."

"We were at the gym when we got the texts," Irish said. "Claire got a text as well."

"Have you checked with anyone else on the team?" Sting Ray read the message again, his gut clenching.

"Only the three of us and Claire got the text." Irish whipped out of the parking lot and back onto the road. "Tuck is concerned. He wants us to meet him at the war room on base."

"Who would send something out like that?" Sting Ray asked. "And how did they get all of our numbers?"

"Dude, what do the four of us have in common?" Big Bird asked, his gaze narrowing.

"We were all in Ethiopia when we stormed the biological weapons factory," Sting Ray said. His eyes

5

widened. "Damn."

"Yeah. Damn." Irish shot a glance in the rearview mirror. "As soon as I got the message, I called Claire. So far, she's okay, but I'm worried about her. If whoever was involved in the manufacturing of the biological weapons has access to some of the virus they were producing, we could be in a lot of trouble."

"Along with the people we care most about," Big Bird added. "Now that we know it's just those who were responsible for destroying the lab, we know who's targeted."

"We know who they want to hurt, but we don't know who they'll hurt that we might care about," Sting Ray said. "You're assuming it will be your women."

Irish and Big Bird both nodded.

"Neither of us have family left," Irish said. "Other than the other members of SEAL Team 10, all we have are our women."

"What about you?" Big Bird asked. "You've never mentioned any family that I know of."

"And you don't have a woman," Irish added.

Sting Ray snorted. "Thanks for the reminder. You're making me sound pathetic."

"No, actually, you're lucky." Irish's brows dipped. "I'm worried about Claire. She's not a trained warrior. She's a doctor. She's vulnerable."

"At least, Yasmin knows not to trust anyone and she's trained to take care of herself." Big Bird's fists bunched. "But against an unknown force, she'll be at risk, as well."

"So, do you have someone you're close to?" Irish asked.

An image of a grizzled mountain man flashed in Sting Ray's mind. "The only person I have left that I can call family is my Uncle Fred."

"Uncle Fred?" Big Bird frowned. "I don't remember you ever talking about him."

"Wait." Irish looked at him in the rearview mirror. "Is he the man you go hunting with every fall when we're not on a mission?"

Sting Ray nodded.

"Doesn't he live in Montana, or somewhere up that direction?"

Again, Sting Ray nodded and a knot settled in his belly.

Irish shook his head. "Surely, he's not someone this nut job will be looking for."

"Yeah, most people don't even know where Montana is." Sting Ray snorted. "Much less how to get there."

It was true. Most people didn't want to go to Montana, especially in the winter months when the temperatures got down well below zero. And most people didn't know about the connection Sting Ray had with his Uncle Fred.

His uncle had been the man to raise him when Sting Ray's parents had died in a freak lightning strike while they had been out on one of their weekly date-nights.

"Montana?" Big Bird scratched his chin. "As in Hank "Montana" Patterson's Montana? Is he anywhere close to where your Uncle Fred lives?"

"As a matter of fact, Hank is only about twenty miles from my uncle's cabin in the Crazy Mountains."

"Crazy Mountains?" Big Bird's brows rose.

Sting Ray chuckled. "Yes, the Crazy Mountains are in Western Montana." He shook his head. "I don't think anyone would go after my Uncle Fred."

"And you don't have a girlfriend hidden somewhere we don't know about?" Irish pressed.

Sting Ray gave them a wry grin. "You know the only ones getting any around here, are you two. If I didn't think you guys were serious about this being a real threat, I'd swear you were looking for a way to rub it in about you having women and me... not so much."

"Believe me, this is one of those times I wish I didn't have a woman in my life. I hate to think of her being in trouble because of me." Irish pulled into his apartment complex.

Sting Ray unbuckled his seat belt and reached for the door handle. "Couldn't it all be a hoax?"

"Are you willing to blow it off and pretend it's a really bad joke someone's playing on us?" Big Bird asked. He shook his head. "I can't imagine anything happening to Yasmin."

"Or Claire," Irish added.

Or Uncle Fred.

How long had it been since he'd touched base with his uncle?

The man lived in a remote cabin in the mountains. He'd only recently acquired a telephone, after years of living without one. The only reason he had a telephone was because Sting Ray had paid to have the lines and poles installed.

Uncle Fred had insisted he had no use for a telephone, but the stubborn old coot had grudgingly agreed to let it stay, once he'd realized he could talk to Sting Ray whenever he liked. The phone wouldn't chop wood and it wouldn't feed his livestock, which were Fred's criteria for usefulness. But he did like to talk to Sting Ray at least once a month. Granted, the conversations were short. Uncle Fred was a man of very few words.

Sting Ray pulled his cell phone from his pocket.

"You calling your uncle?" Big Bird asked.

"Yeah."

Big Bird and Irish nodded, watching Sting Ray as he held the phone to his ear.

Ring. Ring.

Sting Ray's grip tightened.

Ring. Ring.

"No answer?" Big Bird asked.

Sting Ray's lips thinned. He didn't want to get worried yet. His uncle could be out tending to his cattle. Although at 6:30 in the morning on the east coast, it would only be 4:30 AM in Montana. He could be up that early. If he was, he'd be making coffee and would have heard the phone ring.

"Give it five minutes in case he's in the shower or something." Irish pulled into the parking lot of his apartment. "We'll be right back with Claire and Yasmin."

Irish and Big Bird climbed down from the truck and entered the apartment building.

9

Sting Ray counted the seconds, trying to wait the five minutes. At three, he dialed his uncle's number again.

The phone rang. It rang again. Then someone picked up. The sound of something crashing against the wooden floor filled Sting Ray's ear.

"Uncle Fred!" he called out. He waited and then tried again, only louder, "Uncle Fred!"

Someone grunted and coughed. Then the sound of the phone's hard plastic casing bumping across the floor preceded the hoarse croak of someone obviously very sick.

"God damn," Uncle Fred said, his voice barely recognizable. Then came more crackling of plastic against hardwood.

"Uncle Fred, this is Sting Ray. What's wrong with your voice?"

"Sicker than a mangy dog." He coughed into the phone.

Sting Ray's gut knotted and a cold chill slithered across the back of his neck. "How long have you been sick?"

"Just today."

"I'm going to call 911."

"Don't. I'll get over it." He coughed again, sounding like he would hack up a lung in the process.

"Are you in bed?"

"I was."

"Where are you now?"

"On the goddamn," he coughed, "floor."

"Can you stand?"

"No. Just want to sleep. Call later." His voice faded with every word.

"I'm calling the ambulance," Sting Ray said.

His uncle didn't respond. The phone clattered against wood, probably hitting the floor again.

"Uncle Fred!" All Sting Ray could hear was raspy breathing, almost as if his uncle was gurgling.

He hated to hang up, but he did and dialed 911.

When the dispatcher answered, he didn't give her time to say How may I help you. Sting Ray said, "This is Ray Thompson. My uncle, Fred Thompson, lives in Eagle Rock, Montana. I was on the phone with him just now, when I think he passed out."

"I can contact dispatch at Eagle Rock and have them check on your uncle," she offered.

Sting Ray gave her the address to his uncle's place. "One more thing—and this is important— I'm a Navy SEAL just back from a mission involving a dangerous virus. I think someone might have infected my uncle with that virus. When the EMTs go in, tell them it's imperative that they go in prepared with biohazard protective gear."

She assured him that she would pass on all the information. Then she ended the call.

Sting Ray flung open the door, stepped down from the truck and paced back and forth, trying to think of what else he could do. His mind spun around the possibilities.

About that time, Big Bird, Irish and their women arrived at the truck.

Big Bird was first to ask, "What happened?"

"I got ahold of my uncle." Sting Ray stopped

pacing and looked Big Bird in the eyes. "He's sick. Really sick."

"What's he doing for it?" Irish asked.

"Not a damn thing." Sting Ray clenched both fists. "I called 911. They'll transfer the information to the dispatch in Eagle Rock and have an ambulance sent out."

"Did you tell them your uncle could be sick with a deadly virus?" Irish's woman, Claire Boyette, asked. "Do they know to go in with protective gear?"

Sting Ray nodded. "I did." He shook his head. "It's not enough. I need to be there."

Irish touched his arm. "We'll get you home. In the meantime, Montana is there."

Sting Ray stared at Irish, trying to understand his friend and teammate when all he could think about was his uncle, possibly dying alone in his secluded cabin in the fucking backwoods of Montana.

"Focus, Ray." Irish gripped his arms. "Hank Patterson is out there. You said so yourself that he was in the same neck of the woods." He glanced over his shoulder at Big Bird.

Big Bird nodded. "Calling." He pulled his cell phone from his pocket and punched the screen.

Hank Patterson was their teammate who'd left active duty to help his failing father and his new fiancé manage their ranches in Montana.

"I'll put a call in to my boss and get them working on who might be responsible for this threat," Yasmin Evans said. As an agent for the

CIA, she would have contacts all over the world. Surely they could help find the bastard responsible for the notes and, potentially, for infecting his uncle with a highly deadly virus.

Until now, Sting Ray had believed his uncle was invincible. Despite his lack of affection, the man had always been there for him. When Sting Ray's parents had died in a car crash when he'd only been twelve, his uncle had stepped up to the plate and raised him as his own. Loving or not, the man was Sting Ray's only family. He couldn't lose him.

Sting Ray pushed past Irish and stood beside Big Bird.

"Montana, Big Bird here. Sorry to wake you. We've got an emergency and need your help." He paused.

Leaning close to Big Bird's phone, Sting Ray strained to hear the conversation.

"Need you to check on Sting Ray's uncle, Fred Thompson."

"Now?" Hank's voice carried enough Sting Ray could hear.

"Yeah," Big Bird said. "Sting Ray called him a minute ago. He was really sick and must have passed out before the call ended."

"Did you call an ambulance?" Hank asked.

"It should be on the way," Big Bird said. "But that's not all."

No longer able to stand on the sidelines, Sting Ray took the phone from Big Bird. "Hank, this is Sting Ray. We think my uncle might be the target of someone who has threatened retribution on us by harming the people we care about."

Big Bird took the phone back. "Sting Ray's the only one of us who hasn't got a girlfriend. His uncle is his only living relative."

"I'll check on him," Hank promised. "He still lives in that cabin in the Crazy Mountains where we went hunting last fall?"

With his head against Big Bird's hand, Sting Ray heard Hank's question and nodded. "Yeah," he spoke loudly enough for Hank to hear. "But be careful. If he is infected with that virus, you don't want to bring it back to your wife and new baby."

"Thankfully, they're in California right now. But you're right. I'll take precautions. If I don't go, I'll be sure to send someone who can. We'll handle it and let you know."

Irish took the phone from Big Bird. "Hey, Hank. Irish here. We're coming that way, no matter what. If someone did this to Sting Ray's uncle, he might still be there. We'll let you know our flight details as soon as we know them."

"One of my guys has a sister who works for the CDC," Hank said. "I think she's here on vacation. I'll see what I can do to engage her and the CDC on this. If the virus spreads, there's no telling how many more people will be impacted." Hank's voice was lower and harder. It was his community at stake.

"Be careful out there," Irish said. "I'd stay away from town, and drink bottled water for the time being, just in case."

"That'll be really hard to do. We have the

annual rodeo in town and I'm helping out with a chuck wagon."

Sting Ray leaned close to the phone. "For the sake of your wife and daughter, be extremely careful."

"Yeah," Irish said. "I saw what it did to an entire village. Not a soul survived."

"I read you, loud and clear," Hank said. "Believe me, I don't want anything to happen to Sadie or Bella."

Irish ended the call and handed the cell phone to Big Bird. "We've done all we can from here. Let's talk with the boss man and get clearance to go to Montana."

"What about us?" Claire said.

"You're coming, too." Irish slipped his arm around her. "I don't want you out of my sight for a moment." He leaned down and pressed a kiss to her forehead.

Big Bird glanced at Yasmin.

"I'm going, too," Yasmin said. "Maybe if we're in a small town, we'll have a better chance of luring the bad guy and smoking him out."

Big Bird pulled Yasmin into his arms. "Think your boss will let you go?"

She nodded. "If he doesn't, I'll go AWOL." She smiled up at him. "I wouldn't miss this for the world. And I need to keep an eye on you. You might be just as much of a target as Sting Ray's uncle."

Big Bird kissed her on the lips.

Sting Ray's heart pinched. He had to admit,

seeing his friends with their women made him wonder if he should give love another try.

Then he remembered how hard it hurt the first time he'd loved and lost.

He shook his head. Love wasn't for him. Especially not now. He had enough on his plate with a terrorist on the loose sporting a virus that, if it spread, could kill the entire population of the United States.

Also by Elle James

Covert Cowboys Inc Series
Triggered (#1)
Taking Aim (#2)
Bodyguard Under Fire (#3)
Cowboy Resurrected (#4)
Navy SEAL Justice (#5)
Navy SEAL Newlywed (#6)
High Country Hideout (#7)
Clandestine Christmas (#8)

Billionaire Online Dating Series
The Billionaire Husband Test (#1)
The Billionaire Cinderella Test (#2)

Devil's Shroud or Deadly Series
Deadly Reckoning (#1)
Deadly Engagement (#2)
Deadly Liaisons (#3)
Deadly Allure (#4)
Deadly Obsession (#5)
Deadly Fall (#6)

Lords of the Underworld
Witch's Initiation (#1)
Witch's Seduction (#2)
The Witch's Desire (#3)
Possessing the Witch (#4)

Demon Series
Hot Demon Nights (#1)
Demon's Embrace (#2)
Tempting the Demon (#3)

Protecting the Colton Bride
Heir to Murder
Secret Service Rescue
Tarzan & Janine
Haunted
Wild at Heart
Engaged with the Boss
Cowboy Brigade
Time Raiders: The Whisper
Bundle of Trouble
Killer Body
Operation XOXO
An Unexpected Clue
Baby Bling
Nick of Time
Under Suspicion, With Child
Texas-Sized Secrets
Alaskan Fantasy
Blown Away
Cowboy Sanctuary
Lakota Baby
Dakota Meltdown
Beneath the Texas Moon

Printed in the USA
CPSIA information can be obtained
at www.ICGtesting.com
CBHW072220260924
14992CB00008B/318